CUPIDS ESSENCE

J THOMPSON

There are so many people I want to thank for helping me bring Cupid's Essence to life.

Thank you to Stephanie my editor, you my dear rock and you are so stuck with me.

To Yeri, your support means the world to me, more than you can ever know.

To the Chapter chicks and Beta team, Ladies thank you from the bottom of my heart.

Amanda, woman you are amazing.

And finally

To every single reader that pics this story up, remember how amazing you are and never ever doubt it.

Believe in You.

xxx

Prologue

Paris 1825, Midnight

Marcella Rousseau flicked a glance at her locked bedroom door, convinced she had heard a noise. She had hoped the party downstairs would note her absence and would continue long into the night. She continued to watch the door until she was certain there was no sound coming from the other side, before she bent her head back to her task.

She was to leave. Leave everything behind, even her most prized possession; the item that had caused so much turmoil within the past few months, but also the item that had initiated her happiness. She wouldn't leave this most precious of items without writing some instructions for the next owner. Her quill scratched over the parchment as she signed her name, not that they would know who she was but it just felt right. She blew over the ink in an effort to dry it quicker.

A loud, sharp whistle alerted Marcella that her time was up. Ignoring the few smudges on the parchment, she folded it and then pushed it inside a hidden compartment at the back of the rosewood box, along with a small diary. She clicked the door shut and gazed one last time at the contents. The small bottle, so delicate it had literally changed her life and turned it upside down.

"Marcella, my love, you must hurry." Anton's deep voice pulled Marcella from her inner thoughts of the past and the path that had led her to her current situation. She slid the lid closed with a reluctance she fought; she placed the box upon the top shelf of her bookcase. Hiding it within plain sight.

All Marcella had left to do, now, was to take the final leap, trust in her heart and finally follow her dreams. If she stayed, those dreams would be nothing but mists within her mind and as Anton had said on more than one occasion, she was much too stubborn to not live her dreams.

With a lingering look at her shelf, she then turned and walked towards the window. Below lay her future. She placed her foot upon the railing and prepared to take the small jump, knowing Anton would catch her. A small niggling doubt stopped her from stepping off.

"I can't leave it behind," she whispered.

"Marcella, please my darling we have to go, we haven't much time," Anton's voice called, desperation laced his words, shortly followed by a loud bang at her bedroom door, one that shook the room. Marcella ignored the loud, angry voices of the men that had now realised she wasn't present at her own engagement party and looked down at the man that owned her heart. She forgot about the box that she had been so desperate to keep. With a smile she stepped off the balcony and into the open arms of the man meant for her.

Chapter One

"AhChoo!"

Belinda couldn't stop the sneeze that rose from within her sinuses and erupted out of her nose like an F1 car at the start of a race. The force of the sneeze made her stumble forward and she almost ended up face down in a box of old football programmes, the dust and cobwebs very nearly sent her into a fit of sneezing and only her quick movements to get herself back upright stopped it.

"Sorry," she mumbled sheepishly when she realised everyone in the building had turned and looked at her after the eruption. She kept her head down and avoided eye contact. Bloody hell, anyone would think Vesuvius had just erupted the way they were looking at her. Belinda quickly reached into her handbag and grabbed the small pack of tissues that she always carried around. Turning her head, she spotted a small alcove made from bookshelves and stepped into the small space, now hidden amongst the old books, magazines and other bric a brac people liked to sell. She was certain that her cheeks were bright red and it wasn't from the cold either, embarrassment flooded her. Belinda had never been one to want or try to attract attention. She hated having people's eyes on her, watching, so when something like this happened it hit every cell in her body and she had to fight against an anxiety attack. Her only saving grace was the many alcoves, like the one she was stood in.

Carter's Antiques warehouse was an old but gigantic barn that had been converted, about 15 years ago, into a dry storage space. The space held hundreds of small alcoves, run by sellers from all over the country, housing items from pottery all the way to furniture.

Belinda loved it, instead of freezing her arse off like she used to do at antiques fairs or getting piss-wet through because, you know, British weather and all that, she now, thankfully, got to stay dry and take her time perusing to her heart's desire. To her, this place was like what Santa's grotto was to the kids, she had already spent many hours head bent, rifling through boxes to see if she could find treasure.

The old smells that filled the place reminded her of the weekends she used to spend at her grandparents' house; old furniture polish laced with old, flowery scents that tingled the nose and as she had found out, already made her allergies kick off. There was nothing Belinda liked more than spending her Sunday mornings here, buried within the past, away from the craziness of the real world.

Located three miles from her house in Bishops Stortford, it was set in the countryside and not only housed the old barn but also a small tea room, a few craft shops and an outdoor play area for children. In the summer months the farm next door would allow the children to feed the animals, but seeing as it was now February the animals were tucked up and warm, unlike Belinda who had lost the feeling in her toes and finger tips.

She peeked her head out of the alcove and smiled with relief, no one was taking notice of her now and she could continue with her hunt. Panic attack averted.

Her prey, or treasure, were old vintage perfume bottles, ideally the older the better, also, the more ornate the more excited she got. Boasting a collection of 40 bottles, she was proud to say she had a wide range of designs and styles. Some were round and simple and others stood tall and thin, with intricate designs showcasing the skill of those that had produced it. Each one told its own story, gave glimpses into the lives of the previous owners. Her imagination would always go wild when she thought of the times the bottles had come from. She would imagine the ladies all dressed up in beautiful gowns, dabbing their necks with the perfume before sweeping down to meet the gentlemen and find their love, or even attending a secret rendezvous.

Belinda smiled to herself as she dived out of the alcove and continued on her search, she had only been here 25 minutes so she had plenty of time to spare. Sundays were the days she looked forward to most. During the week she worked as a librarian in the local library. She spent her days arranging and sorting books that spoke of love and romance, of adventure and intrigue, and yet, her life was the complete opposite. Her life, although blessed- she was alive and healthy after all- was, in short, boring. Her life consisted of books, perfume bottles and organisation. Belinda was the quintessential spinster. The ones mentioned in the books she loved as having missed out on life and seemed satisfied with their lot, usually chaperoning the lead lady, Belinda thought.

At 28, some would think she was passed it, anyone would think she was 38 the way the old ladies of the town went on. She had been the centre of the gossip in the town ever since she had moved into her grandparents' house and had become the only single, late twenties female in the vicinity. She hadn't missed the comments about how she should just accept it and get a cat. Belinda rolled her eyes and moved towards the next alcove, her eyes flickering over the boxes and shelves.

She knew the trio of Marge, Cleo and Veronica meant well, but their repeated attempts to meddle in her life had started to get very old. She knew they needed entertainment, but trying to set her up with every young man below the age of 30 was getting ridiculous. She might be a virgin but that didn't mean she was desperate.

Belinda had been lucky to have loving and open parents, so it wasn't as if she had been sheltered from life. Yes, she had been born late on in their lives, but every moment had been amazing. They had taught her so much; she had been unlucky to lose them when she was only 25. Her mother had been a gentle soul, unless her father wanted to rile her up. He always knew which button to press and seemed to enjoy doing it. He owned her heart and when she had developed pneumonia, just before her 71st birthday, her father had lasted only six months longer. It hadn't taken much to know that her father had wanted to be with her mum again. The doctors all said his heart had given out, as was expected at the ripe age of 78, but Belinda knew it was more along the lines of a broken heart that had done it. Up until her mother had passed away, her father had been so active he made most young lads look lazy. He cycled every-where, gardened, not only at home, but he also ran his allotment and she never counted the multiple "manly" hobbies he used to do that would drive her mum up the wall. Her parents had adored each other, they never hid it. The secret looks they shared and the loving smiles they openly sported showed a young Belinda that true love was real; you just had to be lucky enough to find the right person to share it with.

Seeing the hint of a sparkle, Belinda headed over towards a particular shiny box full of glass, her mind once again drifting to thoughts of her parents. She knew she was lucky when they had been with her, but after they had gone, she realised just how much. They had always known that the chances of them passing whilst she was still young was high, so they had planned.

When her father had joined her mother, she had been called to the solicitors that had been in charge of their will. They had both been careful with money throughout their lives and had invested well and as such, Belinda had been left with a healthy bank balance, as well as two properties, her parents' home and her grandparents' home. Belinda had been stunned, she had always worked hard and never, ever expected anything like this; her parents had set her up for life.

If she wanted, Belinda could finish work and become a lady of leisure, but what would that leave her with? She had no real friends, unless you classed the lady at the tea room a friend as they were on first name terms. Her job was what stopped her from becoming the spinster the ladies in the town threatened she would be. Her job gave her empty life purpose and got her out of the house and her mind off the fact she was simply lonely, 28 and still single.

Belinda sighed as she moved onto another wooden box filled with bits and pieces made of glass. Her age and relationship was something the 'ladies club' often commented on, acting as if it was a crime. She was sure there were thousands of other women out in the wide world that were the same ages and didn't have men in their lives. But, then again, they probably had friends and social lives. She continued to search through the box; there were beautiful pieces of orange and blue carnival glass, along with lead crystal but, unfortunately, no sign of any perfume bottles.

Belinda continued to slowly move onwards, her mind focusing on the search and no longer on the negatives in her life. At each stall she would smile at the sellers as they looked up from gripping their plastic cups filled with tea or coffee. Some she knew by name and others she had rarely seen as they didn't always man their stalls personally. Most of the time, conversation wasn't really needed when it came to buying her bottles, she wasn't much of a haggler and she would confirm the price and make sure she felt it was worth it, then she would hand over the cash. They probably classed her as a push over but she didn't care. This was her hobby, her love if you could call it that.

Belinda slipped her hands into the warm pockets of her Gilet and started walking again. Regardless of the fact they were inside, it was still colder than a penguin's left nut. The pure size of the building meant that any heat evaporated quickly and no matter what time of year, it was always chilly. She smirked as she walked past a few more of the sellers all huddled around a single oil heater, every single one of them had on a pair of those fingerless gloves and made her think of American based movies like *Home Alone* where the baddies always wore them.

Belinda wandered around for a while longer before deciding she needed a hot drink and a chance to warm herself. The only problem with coming to Carter's was that it was hit and miss; some days she would drop on some of the best bottles she had ever managed to acquire, other times she would leave with nothing but a sniffly nose and an extra slice of the lemon drizzle cake from the café as a consolation prize.

She moved onto the main walkway and headed towards the exit. Her hands had now started to tingle from the cold that in itself told Belinda it was time to go. A cup of tea from the café would sort that out and possibly a bimble around the craft shops would make up for the lack of luck in finding a bottle. Smiling at the final few sellers she stopped and looked at a sign that was stuck to a post in front of an empty alcove. Surely she wasn't that lucky.

Coming soon- Amor Vintage glass- Glass from all over the world

Grinning, she once again headed outside and to the tea room, maybe next week her luck would be in and she would find something unique and stunning.

Chapter Two

Dressed in just a pair of jogging bottoms, the tall, beautifully sculpted male lounged, arms spread wide and legs up on the sofa. If it had been any other male he probably would have looked like a slob, but not this male. His muscles glistened as the sun streamed through the full length windows, the smattering of hair on his chest looked almost golden; a similar shade to the full locks that covered his head, just reaching his chin, it was messy but suited his chiselled features.

His eyes were the colour of the Mediterranean Sea; turquoise depths that hinted at age old knowledge, they mesmerized any who stared into them. This male was utter perfection, a being that could ruin men for all women.

This male was Cupid, and he was bored. He admitted, though only to himself, that it usually didn't take much, but today it seemed nothing would occupy him. Nothing was able to hold his attention, not even the addictively annoying TV show *Jeremy Kyle* that on many occasions would have him chuckling in delight as the mortals aired their troubles and woes so all could see. It amused him and confused him; why did so many mortals have bad teeth? Cupid had assumed, in this modern age, the upkeep of things like teeth and hair would be easy. Cupid shuddered at the thought of these mortals and actually, for a moment, despaired for the future of the human race, before he rolled his eyes and started to flick through the TV channels in search of anything that would take his mind off the fact his wife and goddess, Psyche, had gone off with the other goddess's for a "ladies holiday".

He had no idea what that involved and he didn't want to know. The whims and excesses of one woman was enough to blow anyone's mind, never mind a gaggle of them, and that was before you entered the term goddess into the mix.

So here he was, lonely and bored, with no one to play with. What was a god to do? He stopped briefly from his flicking to watch the tail end of *My Cat from Hell,* letting the thought of '*we should get a cat*' enter his mind, then leave it just as quickly. He didn't have time to deal with an animal pet, hell, he struggled enough with a wife. Cupid snorted at his own joke.

"Ha! Tail… Cat. I'm a funny fucker."

Times had changed, that was obvious, the world of men now had become the world of women too, and that scared him. Once there had been a time a god could find the women wishing for love to fall upon them, now he had to chase them and even then they never seemed to have the time for love. Back in the day, he thought, as he leaned his head back on the soft leather, back in the day mortals would wish and pray with everything they had to have him bestow his unique gift, but now they easily confused comfort and security with the emotion; most settling for only a fraction of what they needed and deserved. The true meaning of soulmates had been lost through time and Cupid felt it to his core. It had been a long time since Cupid had seen a true showing of love, and that inner part of him called out to rectify this.

The minor problem with this was he had sort of been banned from getting personally involved with the mortals. His quest to bring love back into the lives of all had been placed on hold by the one woman who had his nuts in a sack and tied at her waist. She was also the woman he worshipped and loved with every fibre of his being. Pussy-whipped, under the thumb, yes he was and he was damn proud.

That woman was his everything and he was, in

turn, hers. They had a love that transcended time and space and would be still when the world grew old and ceased to be. But, he digressed; he had been banned from interfering with the mortals and after that small, unfortunate event, his dear wife, Psyche, had said some very wise words which he assumed had a point. But as with a lot in life, it went in one ear and out the other. He had been watching *Judge Rinder* at the time.

"You can't force love on all Cupid, my love, you will only, in the end, cause hate and resentment."

This had been said after he had tried to "force" love, and it turned out one side of the relationship had been more smitten with his gardener than the lady that had fought to win his attention and affection. Seemed like Cupid had been blinder than the young lady had been.

So here he sat, still bored and at a loss of what to do. He couldn't directly interfere as that would tighten the strain on his beloved nut sack. So how could he get around this, in a loophole-ish sort of way? Cupid rose from his reclined position and ignored the bits of popcorn and chocolate that dropped to the floor. He stood to his full and powerful six-seven height and stretched his arms above his head as he pushed his hips forward and his back backwards, he groaned with satisfaction as a crack echoed throughout the room.

"Ahhh much better," he called out to no one, his voice low and husky. He followed it with a chuckle as he adjusted himself in his joggers and walked to the full length windows. "Sorry boys, nearly strangled you there." He apologised to his man package, keeping his hand there out of habit and comfort. Who needed a blankie when you had a set like he did?

Cupid focused his attention on the stunning view the large windows afforded him, enjoying the sunshine as it hit the multitude of glass buildings, showing that even the modern could be beautiful.

Psyche had chosen the apartment because she had a love for the old structures in London, she would spend most days wandering around taking in the sights. It was one of the things he loved about her; her excitement at the world, every day, no matter where they were. The city from his point of view looked as it always had, busy with people jostling for position, no time to enjoy the fact they were alive, alive and gifted with the most basic of abilities; to love. The mortals of the world were an impressive race, they had the innate ability to respond and evolve to the constantly changing world around them with little effort, yet, it annoyed him no end how they took those little things for granted.

Lifting his hands and resting them upon the glass, he watched as the sun once again broke through the clouds, highlighting the colours that stood out. He watched as the odd mortal would stop from their haste and lift their head to the sun, eyes closed as they bathed in its heat. Cupid smiled, all was not lost with the mortals and even though he had been told his man card had been revoked, it didn't mean he couldn't get around it.

A plan formulated and percolated in his mind and he laughed. This would solve his boredom, alleviate his need to interfere and all the while, sticking to his wife's rules. He chuckled as he turned from the window and made his way towards the apartment's marble bathroom that housed a full rainforest style shower and a large walk-in tub.

Dropping his joggers, he padded around naked, turning on the water. This was a mortal invention that made his super happy. His grin widened. What would make him even happier would be sending his absent wife a saucy picture before he hatched his plan. Well, he didn't want her forgetting about him and how lonely he was after all, he thought, as he climbed

into the shower to prepare him and *Pedro* for said
picture.

21

Chapter Three

The sound that erupted from Belinda's mouth as she yawned sounded like a Wookie going into battle, but she could do little to stop it besides covering her mouth with her hand and seeing it through. She was- and wasn't- a morning person, she loved to get up and get things done; the only problem was the getting up part. No matter how early she got herself to bed she always felt like she had only got about two hours sleep.

She rubbed her eyes once more, then grumbled, "ah shit." Her make-up, although she didn't wear a lot, would be smudged and she would again have to reapply. She checked her handbag to make sure she had everything she needed, grabbed her lunchbox and her travel mug before she left the house and locked the door.

At 7:15am it was dreary and felt dark. The cold stung her face as she walked to the curb where she had parked her beloved 1968 Volkswagen Beetle, a classic in the most beautiful emerald green, it was her only love. When her grandfather had passed away, her father had put it into storage, not wanting to get rid and in turn, Belinda had got her paws on it. She had, of course, spent a small fortune on getting it refurbished, but every penny had been worth it. It had also given her the best excuse to finally talk to the mechanic that lived a few doors down.

His name was Mike and she thought he was a similar age to her but she had never got round to asking anything personal. She had, unfortunately, lost the ability to form coherent words or sentences when he was around. Add in the cute factor, that he was shy himself and had a slight stutter, it pulled at her heart strings and made her want to hug him, possibly kiss him.

Belinda grinned as she slid the old fashioned key into the ignition, turned once, then pulled out the choke. She waited for the old car to think about starting before she turned again. As expected, her emerald beauty started with a chug.

"Atta girl." Belinda smiled, looked around for other traffic and then pulled off and into the road, waving at Veronica as she passed. The old lady's purple-rinsed curls appeared at the window before a wrinkly hand followed in response to Belinda's wave.

Her thoughts drifted back again to Mike and his blues eyes and dirty blonde hair- well, she assumed it was dirty blonde. He was a mechanic after all, for all she knew he was white blonde, but she had never seen him with freshly washed hair. Her OCD twitched at the thought of him not washing his hair.

"Well that's a put off, right there," she said aloud as she drove through the quiet streets. This time of day, although too early, was so special. The breaking of the day and the start of the new, plus it was a Monday. Belinda loved Mondays, yes, she knew she was a strange phenomenon in the world, but she just did. Mondays were her alone days in the library as Cyril, the other librarian, always had it off. So she could arrange and organise to her heart's content, without the older man watching her. He always had a comment or two to make about her odd habits and the fact no book could be left out of place for longer than four minutes and thirty seconds. Well, that had been the longest she had lasted and it had left Cyril in stitches for well over an hour. Every time he had looked at her, he had started laughing again. If she was honest she adored the man, he had filled a small hole that had appeared when her parents' had died and helped to make her feel, during the day, that she wasn't as alone as she felt during the evening and weekends.

The scenery streaked past as she steered the Beetle through the streets and towards town. The weather seemed to be getting even duller, the temperature was already sitting at eight degrees, but Belinda felt like it was less. She didn't like the cold, in fact, she hated it and in the winter months she would wear as many layers as possible. The first rain drop hit the roof of the car and sounded like a drum that had been placed right by her ear. It was soon followed by a torrential downpour, coupled by thunder that cracked and hinted the weather gods were not happy.

Belinda slowed the car down to a crawl as her visibility reduced to almost zero. The rain poured down the windows. This was strange, she thought, as she recognised the part of the road where she could turn off and park. Her windscreen wipers went back and forth at high speed and she was worried that they would fly off at any moment.

She pulled into the town car park and parked in her favourite spot, but right now it wasn't feeling as fabulous as it usually did. It sat directly under a large oak tree, its base a good two meters around. It was said it had been planted back when the town was first birthed. Regardless of how old it was, Belinda would not be impressed if the storm chose this tree to knock down, straight onto her car. Pursing her lips, she turned the car back on and manoeuvred it into another space free from the chance of any tree or building from falling onto it.

She sat there as the rain continued to pummel the car, watching as the rivulets of water flowed down the windscreen and made rainbow patterns in the light of every streak of lightening. The patterns forming entranced her, and her mind drifted off to when she was a kid watching the same sort of storm from her bedroom window as her mum told her stories. It was her mum's fault she had become a book lover and in turn, a librarian. Belinda smiled as she remembered her mum taking her to a library for the first time. She had done that mesmerised turn that Belle did in *Beauty and the Beast*, amazed that so many books could be in one place and she still felt that way, even now, when she walked into work.

Looking through the window as it started to steam up, Belinda pulled the strap of her handbag over her head, collected her lunch box and travel mug and moved to open the door, only to let loose a loud scream as she saw a face peering back at her through the glass.

"AAAAAHHHHHHH!"

In response to her scream, the face winced then stepped back so she could open the door, and there, stood in the rain, fulfilling a fantasy Belinda never knew she had, was Mike. Dressed in his overalls that were now very damp, he smiled at her shyly.

"So-So sorry for sc-sc-scaring you." His voice was deep and lulling, even with the stutter. Belinda had to concentrate to answer back with an actual coherent sentence.

"It's ok Mike, sorry for screaming." She smiled back, how could any woman resist a guy dressed in overalls that filled them like Mike did? He had the sleeves rolled up to show off powerful forearms and his biceps, she could see, almost bulged out of the material. His shoulders were huge too, and even though the outfit wasn't classed as flattering, he filled every inch to perfection.

"My-My fault, Be-Belinda, I should have kn-knocked on the window."

Belinda hoisted her handbag back onto her shoulder and attempted to hide the bright purple unicorn lunchbox that she had clutched in her hand. Feeling her cheeks warm, she answered quickly, "It's fine Mike, honest, I should have been more aware of my surroundings." She made the excuse, not wanting him to think he was at fault. He had made her day by just talking to her.

"Can I help you with something?" she asked, not wanting to get to the point of his unexpected visit, but she needed to be in work soon or her internal twitch meter would start and the last thing she wanted was to get snappy at the only guy so far that made her pulse race.

"Oh ye-yes, so so-sorry. The Beetle is almost due its next service." He paused and pushed a large hand through his now soaking locks as the rain had now slowed down. "Do you wan-want me to take it over and get it done for you?"

Wow, Belinda thought, she had totally forgot, which was in itself completely not like her. She frowned as she remembered her calendar and couldn't, not for the life of her, remember a date for the service being on there.

"Are you sure?" she asked, not happy she had forgotten something so important.

"Ye-Yes," he answered, his gorgeous blue eyes watching her, his smile gone and only a small frown marring his face. "Yo-Yo-You don't ha-ha-have to now, we can so-so-sort it another day if you would like."

"No, no, that's fine Mike. I'm sorry, please would you? It means I won't have to worry then." Belinda smiled as she handed over her car keys. Their skin touched briefly before he pulled back his hand and placed it on the frame of the open door.

"I will dro-drop the keys back to you la-la-later then." He smiled once more and Belinda's stomach did that feeling it did when you went on a roller coaster.

"Thank you Mike, so much," she replied, and took the hint to move out of the way so he could enter the car. He gave her one more smile before he folded his large frame into the Beetle and started the engine. Why Belinda stood there watching Mike leave in her car- in the rain no less- she didn't know, but there was something about Mike that made Belinda want to watch him. She would admit it would be better if he was butt naked though. The innocent side of her brain, the one that had kept her a virgin for so long, gasped in outrage and shouted "you hussy". Belinda could only grin, she may be innocent but she wasn't blind.

†

At 12pm Belinda cracked open her bright purple lunch box and smiled at the sight of one delicious salami, mayo and pickled onion sandwich. This was her favourite combo, even beating a crisp butty. The day had been a good one so far and she had Mike to thank for that. He had started the day well and so far, things had been going to plan. All returns had been catalogued and filed back into place, postal orders had been scanned and packaged ready to go the next day, the desk had been reorganised after the mess the Saturday girl had left and she had enjoyed a Costa, which had been bought to her by Veronica on her way back from her shopping trip in town.

She had left the radio on the entire morning, letting the calming sounds of Classical FM fill the office. She had only a few visitors who had requested books that needed to be ordered and had to send a few letters out for unpaid charges, but nothing too taxing.

Belinda bit into the sandwich and groaned, then almost choked as someone walked into the library. She hated people seeing her eat at work; she was always afraid she looked like a pig troffing and would rather be seen as professional.

As the figure approached, she realised it was

Mike, but this time instead of the oily overalls, he was dressed in jeans and a long sleeved jumper. Belinda had to force the piece of bread down her gullet as she stared. Mike looked hot in overalls, but in this outfit… Belinda was close to either drooling or swooning. She knew he had a big build, hell, you couldn't miss it with the size of him, but she never actually realised that most of it was muscle. The stereotypical build of a mechanic, in her head, was one with some arm strength, but with a bit of a belly. She couldn't help it and that's how a lot of people saw them. But not Mike, from what she could see as he walked closer, was that every bulge was muscles; from huge biceps to well defined pecs. His jeans sat low on his hips but they weren't those god awful skinny jeans that some men chose to wear, no, they were the loose fit, which looked bloody amazing.

"Hi Be-Belinda." He smiled, his eyes shining with humour, as if he knew she had been checking him out. She stood and smiled back, but inside she was cursing her smelly salami and pickled onion sandwich. Typical, Mike visits and she's about as approachable as a pig sty with her stinky breath.

Trying not to breathe out too much, she replied, "Hi Mike, I almost didn't recognise you without your overalls on."

"I-I-I've just finished and ha-have the afternoon off." He smirked and held out his hand, a part of her- that hussy part- thought he wanted to take her hand, before she realised he was giving her the car keys back.

"The Be-Be-Beetle is run running like a dr-dream."

Belinda nodded. "Awesome, thank you so much, have you got the invoice?" She took the keys and turned to grab her handbag from the office. "How much do I owe you?" Again, her hussy side responded in her head with an offer of bodily payment. Belinda rolled her eyes at herself, she would need some sort of medication soon to control the slut that had appeared in her head. Maybe, if she just got rid of her virginity it would stop annoying her with innuendos and inappropriate comments when she didn't need or want them. His voice stopped her from pulling out her purse.

"No-No-No charge, my tr-treat," he called out as he started to walk back to the front door of the library. "Buy me a dr-drink sometime."

Belinda tilted her head and watched him leave; he seemed eager to go and wouldn't have heard her answer, even if she had given one. But he had left, leaving her with a sight that would now, and always, be burned onto her retinas. There it was! An arse so peachy it filled the denim as if god herself (yes god was female) had cupped it around the cheeks and drafted it for his arse alone. Belinda sighed and turned to the laptop, bringing up Google. With quick fingers she typed in her first search of the afternoon: 'How to exorcize a sex freak'.

†

Mike sat behind the wheel of his Toyota Hilux and banged his head on the wheel. He hated his stutter, but today he loathed it even more. No matter how calm he tried to be it always went bloody crazy when he spoke to Belinda. He had known her for a few years now, known as in, they had been neighbours. He had helped her move in and had always said hi on passing, until the day she had asked him about her classic Beetle. He didn't think she had realised that when she had first brought it to the garage, the lads that had worked there had immediately been smitten with her, and, for a second, he had regretted telling her where he worked.

He had found her instantly stunning and he knew she wasn't like other women. He had never seen her with female friends, unless he counted the blue rinse trio that he had seen her talking to on occasion, and she didn't seem as flaky as other women he had met. She was intelligent, that was obvious, but she also hinted at some issues that made admitting his own easier. He had overheard the trio talking about her a lot; she seemed to be the focus of their conversations most of the time. They had mentioned she lived on her own since her parents had passed away and that she wasn't a drinker or a heavy party animal; she preferred a good book and a cosy night in. Mike liked the sound of that.

He smiled and remembered the times he had seen Belinda buried behind a book in her garden and would, again, admit he had watched her. Yes, she was his crush, but he felt she was so far out of his league it was like watching Braintree United take on Chelsea in the FA cup final. Everyone knew the result would be one way, but it didn't stop them believing.

He had approached her today in the hopes of maybe asking her out, but when he had scared her he had chickened out and made up the bullshit about her car needing a service. He knew she had issues with organising and slight OCD, so when she had got twitchy he had back tracked, but he had been thankful when she had agreed. Her car ran perfect and he had done it for free. His boss had known the minute he had driven the car into the garage and he had been subjected to a morning of piss taking. It had been lucky he had booked the afternoon off so he could see a physio. He had decided that morning to try and catch her before work and the fact he had to drop her keys off had fitted in with perfection, in theory that was.

The plan had been made in his head, just executing it had been the biggest issue; walk in, give her the keys and then say "want to go for a drink", only that never left his lips. Instead, he had to battle his stutter the entire time and in the end, had bolted out of the door leaving only a small note tucked in her planner he had seen laid out on the desk.

Mike leaned back in his seat and tapped his palms on the wheel. When had asking a girl out become so damn hard? It had never been this difficult when he had been younger.

Slamming his hand onto the wheel again, he started the engine. His consolation prize was the look on her face when she had seen him out of his overalls. He knew he looked alright in the body department. Twice weekly rugby training, coupled with gym time meant he was healthy and looked good. He grinned, he wasn't cocky about it, he just knew it. And the fact a few ladies had mentioned it, along with the lads at work making remarks, calling him the local Hulk. He didn't mind, he enjoyed keeping fit and healthy, as well as knocking the shit out of the lads when playing rugby. If he happened to look good whilst doing it, he wasn't about to complain, and if the look on Belinda's face was anything to go by, it was worth every god damn bead of sweat, bruise and busted nose.

He slotted the truck into gear and pulled out of his space at the back of the garage. His physio appointment wasn't for another half hour, but he never expected to be such a pussy and back out of talking to Belinda. He dreaded both her agreeing to meet him for a drink and her not answering his message.

Reaching down, he grabbed a mint from the centre console and grinned when he thought back to her choice of lunch and lunch box. She may act all prim and proper, but she had quirky and unique tastes. He had sworn he had smelled pickled onions when he had walked up to the desk, and her face had looked like she had been busted doing something she wasn't meant to.

His grin quickly turned into a wince as he remembered his appointment. His physio was neither relaxing nor gentle, it was more along the lines of minor torture. Focusing on the road, he dreaded what was about to happen; that he was about to be put through a world of pain by his physio to sort his back out from his last rugby game.

Yes, this was certainly going to hurt.

Chapter
Four

Belinda walked through her front door, kicked it closed and dropped her bags. Turning her head to the left, she was faced with her reflection, her soaking wet, mascara smudged, red faced reflection. The weather was supposed to have been dry all day but, of course, decided to chuck it down the minute she had to get some shopping. She'd had to lug all the heavy bags from down the road to her house, causing her now drowned rat look. All because some muppet had parked in her usual space outside her home.

With a sigh she pushed the wet strands from her face and dumped her keys on the small table that was beneath the ornate mirror. So instead of coming in and getting the dinner on, in her usual regular routine, she would instead be sorting her damp self out, as well as drying her wool coat to make sure it didn't ruin. Most people would have just dumped it on the hook but Belinda couldn't physically do that. The mere idea that she had left something like that and it could possibly start to smell or get ruined gave her palpitations.

Belinda picked up her shopping bags and took them into the small kitchen. Being in an old town-house meant the kitchen was at the back of the house and was one of the smallest rooms. But she liked it. There was enough room for a two-seater table near the back door so she could look out onto the garden when she ate her breakfast. She placed the bags on the counter and then put the food packets away in the fridge and cupboards. Everything had its place and had to be sorted straightaway.

She draped her coat over the back of a chair and placed her handbag on the table, she needed her phone so she could google how to deal with a damp wool coat. Google had been her saviour more times than not. Typically, she could never find her phone when she needed it. She pulled out her tissues, make-up bag, perfume, purse, coin purse, kindle and then her planner, setting them next to each other on the table before she headed back into the craterous bag for a second look.

"Got you, bloody slippery thing," she called out loud and fished her iPhone from the bottom. She stopped as she noticed a pink piece of paper wedged into her planner on the table. She never wedged anything into her planner; anything she did put in there was always neatly placed inside to await being dealt with. It was strange as she hadn't made any notes this week, her planner had been up to date on Monday and she had known what was happening by heart as it was a quiet week.

Her phone and Google forgotten, she picked up the planner and took out the battered, pink post-it note. The writing was not hers and was legible, although a little messy. She had never seen the writing before, so at first, was very confused as to how and why it was in her planner.

Can I buy you a drink tonight? My number is 07789 454 781

Mike

What the hell? Belinda thought. Mike had asked her out! Yes, it had been on a note, but he had asked her out! Belinda closed her eyes and thought back to the last time she had seen Mike; he had returned her keys after he had taken her Beetle for a service. That had been a few days ago. She had, in his eyes, ignored his message.

"Bollocks," she cursed, pulling out a chair before slumping into it. She bet he thought her to be an uptight cow now and would probably avoid her in the future.

A smile formed as she thought back to the day she had seen Mike at the library. She had found his stuttering so cute and had noted he seemed on edge as well as looking hot as hell in his jeans and top. He must have slipped the note inside her planner when she had turned to grab her purse and had made his escape soon after. But that just brought another memory to the forefront of her mind: the day they had met. Belinda would never forget it.

Oh god, she had looked awful, just like she had today. It hadn't been long after her parents had passed away and she had made the decision to move to the property that had been left to her by her grandparents.

It was a day just like this one; wet, dismal and depressing, which had made her mood even worse. Grief is a unique emotion and changes with each and every person it consumes. For her, all she had wanted was to vanish in her books and work and not see a soul.

In her emotional state, Belinda had forgotten the need for a removals company and had to settle for lugging numerous boxes and furniture into the house herself. The rain had hammered against the pavement and on every trip she had become increasingly drenched until even her underwear was soaked through. And that had been how Mike had found her, on the front step to her house, the contents of her precious memory box littered across the entrance and tears streaming down her face.

There had been pictures of when she was a child playing on the beach with her dad, horse riding with her mum and snippets of their busy but happy lives. She had watched, dumbstruck, as a man she had never met before had just smiled and then bent to collect the pictures, before placing them inside the damaged box and had then started to collect the rest of the broken contents.

In that one moment, Belinda had given a part of her heart to him. It didn't matter that she didn't know his name at the time, or that he could have had an ulterior motive. All that had mattered was he had simply smiled and then helped her instead of asking what was wrong. It was like he had known then and there that if he had asked, she would have erupted into a storm of emotion that wouldn't have been easy to stop.

He had stood there getting soaked to the bone

and just smiled, it wasn't a cocky smile either, it was an understanding smile that said it was ok and he would help. And he had, he had helped her finish up moving all of her things from the car and then she had made them both a cup of tea. She had then found out that he was a mechanic and, in turn, they had talked about her little classic Beetle.

Mike had been there when she had been convinced she had no one left in the world.

Belinda wiped her face of the tears that had escaped at the memory of their first meeting. It was amazing how such a simple act could cement a person in your heart. But it had, and he had remained there ever since, not that he knew, nor would he ever until she had gained enough courage to broach the subject.

Belinda came back to the present and immediately felt awful. He would think she hadn't bothered to call or message him because she didn't want a drink, when that was far from the truth. She looked at the phone in her hand then back to the paper with Mike's surprisingly neat scawl across it, in seconds she had saved it to the memory. She wouldn't message him yet. She had to compose a message that didn't sound too desperate or stupid and portrayed how sorry she was that she hadn't messaged him that night, or since. The possibility she had blown any chance of seeing Mike on a more regular basis gave her slight anxiety. Belinda had always prided herself on being a kind and honest person, and the thought of someone thinking ill of her actions because she could be forgetful didn't sit well at all.

She left her handbag and its contents spread out on the table, switched the cooker on and walked out into the hall and up the stairs, she had started to dither due to still being soaked through from the rain. She would have a nice hot shower, sort the wool coat out, eat and then sit down to send the message. Only then would she be able to switch off from the week and ready herself for the weekend. Carter's had advertised that they were holding a special antiques festival this weekend, so Belinda wanted to be there bright and early the next morning.

†

The shower had been wonderful; the warmth had slowly seeped into her bones and made her feel more human once again. She had put her clothes into wash, had eaten a delicious meal of chicken in a white sauce, with rice and veg, and now sat on the sofa curled up with her laptop once again googling how to deal with a wool coat. That was the last time she bought one. With the British weather being so unpredictable, she would have to get one of those warm and cosy TOG coats, but they didn't quite go with her work outfit.

Luckily, she hadn't trashed the coat. It had been a good job she hadn't stuffed it into the dryer when she had got in or else she could have had a coat that would have fitted one of her mum's porcelain dolls. She had done exactly the right thing by hanging it up in the utility room and letting it air dry. She just hoped the rank smell would vanish as it dried; it currently reminded her of the old man that ran Carter's, the one with the protruding front tooth and food down his trousers.

Everything in the house had been sorted and her OCD, for now, was under control. Well, it was until she remembered the unanswered message and that she needed to reply to Mike.

Her anxiety started to show then, making her hot and sweaty as she reached for her phone and brought up a blank message and… just sat and looked at it. Flashbacks of not being able to talk to the boys at school hit her, along with the memories of realising they weren't the most important thing in her life.

One boy, who had been Mr popular and who had all the girls after him, had approached Belinda after

PE one day; she had still been dressed in her navy blue netball skirt and bright green t-shirt and had thought she had gone to heaven. He had stood next to her, saying how much he thought she was brilliant at netball. Which, she was of course. But things had soon taken a turn when he had started to try and lift her netball skirt and then she had heard the laughter of the boys around the corner. She had been a dare and a practical joke.

Well! She grinned at the thought; the joke, in the end, had ended up on him. Her father had always taught her to not put up with bullies, so she had done the first thing to pop into her head. She had grabbed his wrist from lifting her skirt and, as her dad had taught her, bent his wrist backwards before slamming the heel of her other hand into his nose.

He had hit the deck in a flood of tears and blood, and she had been sent to the headmaster's office and her parents called. That was the day she had known she didn't fit in with the other kids and had decided to focus on being herself. It was a hard lesson to learn at 11, but it had served her well in life so far.

She had kept her guard up when it came to men, which was one of the reasons why she was still a virgin. It wasn't that she didn't like them, she just knew that the moment she slept with a man she would become emotionally compromised to them, and in turn, they had the power to hurt her. It was a daft notion and could mean she would go through life not experiencing that most powerful of acts, but she would rather protect her heart than have an orgasm. She had lost too much to risk putting herself though that kind of pain all because she had been a crap judge of character. Yes, she was most likely being a fool in waiting and hoping on finding someone that would take her, quirks and all. Though, a part of her had hoped Mike would be the one. Well, that was before she had blown it. Biting her lip to stop herself from twitching, she started to type.

Mike.

Hi it's Belinda. I wanted to apologise for not messaging you sooner. I have only just found your note in my planner. Please believe me, it wasn't deliberately missed.

She paused and read it back. Did it sound pathetic? She just wanted to be honest, but sometimes her honesty made her sound worse. She blew out a breath and continued on, her fingers flying over the screen.

I am so very sorry if I have let you down in any way.
    Belinda.

She kept it short and simple, not wanting to waffle on as she would like. After hitting send, she placed her phone down and looked back to her laptop before shutting it down and putting it away. She would make a hot drink, then go to bed and read a few chapters of a book before heading to sleep. Tomorrow was another day and would hopefully be a good one.

Chapter Five

Mike rolled over and groaned; his head felt like someone had pierced it with an axe. The pain came in waves, over and over, the crescendo of each one nearly sending him back into bed. He had to get up, had little choice, in fact. He had to be up and dressed, ready to drive his mate, Gary, to their rugby game today. Why he had gone out last night he didn't know, usually when he had a game he would stay in and get an early night. But the lads at work had persuaded him that he needed some time out of the house and to see what the world had to offer. He snorted and then winced, he had foolishly told them he had given "the librarian" his number, and when she had never texted back they had taken the piss, but also offered to introduce him to ladies that would appreciate him more. Those ladies had most definitely not been his type and he had sat in the corner of the bar getting quietly drunk until Stuart, his boss, had offered to take him home.

He had been shocked that Belinda had never messaged him, even to turn him down. He had always thought her to be nice and not stuck up, but her actions were now changing his mind. He would have preferred a message of rejection, at least then he knew where he stood. Was it his stutter that made him such a turn off, or did she think she was better than him because he was just a mechanic and she was a snooty librarian?

The more he had thought about it and the more he drank, the more pissed off he had become. But now he cupped his head in his hands as he sat on the side of his bed, still dressed in the clothes from the night before. Now he was paying for it, his head hurt, he felt sick as a dog and he smelled bad. The smelling bad part must have been from the drink launched his way when he had mentioned that all women were the same and were not to be trusted. Yeah, women don't take man rants well and he had been given a glass full of Baileys in the face to prove it.

Mike stood up, slowly stripped off and then headed across the hall and into the bathroom. He turned the water on for the shower and turned up the heat. It would be hot enough to take a layer of skin off, but he didn't care, he would do anything to clean off the excesses of last night and attempt to make him feel slightly better.

Most weekends he would already be at work, but for certain games he had booked the days off or had put in some overtime so he could have the day off. He was looking forward to the game, it offered a way of getting out any pent up frustration, and it also meant hammering the shit out of the other players. He would no doubt end up straight back in his current position; running a shower hot enough to blister skin as he washed away the game, revealing every bruise and scratch.

He climbed into the shower and groaned out loud as the water hit his bare skin. Steam soon filled the room and leaked out into the hall from the open door, but Mike didn't care. He wished he could spend longer under the heated water but he knew Gary would be arriving any time now, and the last thing he needed was his best mate walking in on him in the shower. It had happened before and was horrific enough that a repeat was to be avoided. He could still remember the awkward silence and avoided eye contact that occurred in the weeks after.

Making quick work of cleaning up, he turned the water off and quickly hopped out and grabbed a towel from the rail. Wrapping it around his hips, he ignored the wet marks he left on the wood flooring and returned back to his room. His eyes caught sight of his phone on the floor, left from where he had thrown it the night before. Knowing it would be dead he plugged it in then continued to grab his gear for the day, making sure to pack a change of clothes for after the match. Because the weather had been wet of late, he added an extra towel. Luckily, he still had a bin bag in there from last time. Rugby was a messy game after all, and he may be a male but he wasn't completely useless.

Once Mike was dressed in some comfy joggers and a loose jumper, he pushed his hands through his hair in an effort to control the locks. He knew he was overdue a cut but he just couldn't be bothered to get it done.

"MIKE!!" a voice called from downstairs. Gary had arrived and, of course, had made himself at home. The smell of bacon and coffee had him throwing his stuff into his bag quicker than usual. Hoisting it over his shoulder, he headed down the stairs, forgetting his phone in the process.

"I brought the essentials as you are driving," Gary called out as Mike walked down the stairs and dumped his bag by the door, next to Gary's. "I got bacon and egg baguettes with tommy K, two large coffees from Costa and a collection of tasty pastries for the journey from Tesco." He grinned as he waved an arm over the goodies on the table.

"Nice one man, I'm starving," Mike answered, reaching for his baguette. If he didn't eat soon he was convinced his stomach would rebel and start eating itself. That was his own fault for not eating at all before he had starting drinking the night before.

"You hungry then dude?" Gary asked, and was gifted with an energetic nod, followed by a wince. Mike would need painkillers before the match. It would help in case anyone clocked him in the head during the match.

"You feeling rough? Coz you bloody look it dude. I thought you didn't drink before a match."

Mike shrugged then answered, "The lads from work wanted to go out and I thought, what the hell."

Gary sat and started to devour his own breakfast. They sat in silence as they both chewed before Gary asked, "She never replied, did she?"

Mike glared over at Gary but never answered his question. He didn't want to talk about the fact Gary knew he'd had a crush on Belinda for a long time and had put off asking her out due to the very reason he got drunk. Mike had never handled rejection well and he hated talking about it even more. After finishing his food, he tossed the rubbish into the bin and walked out of the kitchen, grabbing his jacket from the bannister.

"Come on or else we will be late," he called to Gary as he picked up his bag from the floor. "Bring the coffee and munchies," he finished as he walked out the door and onto the pavement. He stopped short as he watched Belinda, dressed in a pair of faded blue jeans and a warm jacket, climb into her Beetle. He continued to watch as she pulled away from the curb and drove up the road.

For fuck sake, what was it about her that had him entranced even when she had made it obvious that she wasn't interested?

"You have it bad dude."

"Fuck off and give me a pastry," Mike growled out as he walked towards his truck.

Chapter Six

Belinda buzzed with excitement as she jostled her way into the packed building of Carter's. Because it was classed as an antiques festival, hundreds of people had rocked up, along with lots of new stalls. This excited Belinda, she had been disappointed last weekend when she had found nothing and she hoped with the new stalls she would at least find a few pieces to add to her collection.

She stopped to let an old woman wobble past and felt her phone vibrate within her pocket. Ever since she had sent the message to Mike she had been on edge, waiting for a reply. She hadn't expected one right away, but the longer it was left the more she was convinced that she had completely blown it.

Her hands shook as she took her phone from her pocket and unlocked the screen, bringing up the recent messages. Her shoulders sagged as she read the message from Veronica, one of the trio of ladies that you could call her friends.

Bel honey

Have a fab day at the fair. Have signed you up to EHarmony!!!

Could you feed Bubbles tonight? I'm off out to the bingo and Clark will be there.

Looks like I'm in.

Much love

Ronnie

Belinda frowned and replied back that she would indeed feed Bubbles and to have a good night. She would not get into a row about being signed up to a dating site, well not yet anyway. She would broach that subject of dating websites when she next went over and saw the trio. She knew all three of them had done it, and no matter how many times she protested she was positive it went in one ear and out the other. She read back through Veronica's message and she could swear that woman had been taking lessons from the teenagers that worked at the bingo house. She sounded younger every time she sent a message.

With a sigh Belinda put her phone back into her pocket and tried to forget the dating site and focus on the here and now. She smiled openly to all the sellers and started to slowly walk around the stalls. She began at the ones that had been at Carter's for years, scared she might actually miss a piece from them, before she would tackle the new sellers.

The atmosphere was amazing and Belinda felt so at home routing through boxes, looking for any piece of glass that was hidden in the hopes of finding that special bottle.

The temperature had picked up, which was why it had been so wet recently, but it also meant that it was slightly warmer in the building, that meant most of the sellers didn't have their funky little gloves on and the heaters weren't needed as much. Besides, the amount of bodies inside the building meant that the body heat alone brought up the temperature, as well as increased the sales.

Having exhausted the existing sellers, Belinda headed over to the new ones in the alcove near the entrance, where the new stall called "Amor Glass" had been advertised. She half expected it to either be not yet set up or to be full of modern day glass ware, but instead it was filled with the most beautiful glass and crystal ware she had ever seen; wine glasses, decanters, bowls and plates sparkled like new and there, like the

Holy Grail for Belinda, was a cabinet filled with perfume bottles.

She was still ten feet away, as she was unable to move through the crowd, but she could see the rainbow colours glisten from the lights. Her heart rate picked up and her palms became clammy. This was the feeling she loved, for her it was the same type of feeling adrenaline junkies got when they jumped off a cliff or out of a plane.

"Excuse me, can I squeeze past?" she called out to two men as they stood discussing a piece of porcelain on another stall, but they had managed to block the walk way. She stood and smiled sweetly, but that soon changed to a frown when they ignored her and continued to stand in the way.

With a louder voice she called again and tapped one of the men on the shoulder.

"Excuse me, can I get past please?"

She watched as he turned and looked down at her and sneered. "Go the other bloody way love, I'm busy." He turned his back on her and continued his conversation about the antique charger plate he had in his meaty hands.

Belinda's eyes widened at his blatant rudeness and she clenched a fist. With a few deep breaths she calmly tapped him on the shoulder again and waited.

"What the fuck do you want now? I told you to go the other way."

Belinda smiled and stepped forward. "That's a fake," she said, and pointed to the plate and then to the seller, who she knew was a complete jackass. "He has them made in China and shipped over."

The potential buyer turned in anger to the seller, whose eyes nearly bulged from his head as he noticed the now furious man slowly stalk towards him. Belinda took the chance to squeeze past the gap that had opened up and headed for the Amor stall. Yes, that had been a bit nasty, but that guy had been an arse and so was the seller. In the past, he had been so rude to her when she had visited his stall, so she saw that as kiss from karma. Plus, if that hadn't of worked she would have resorted to violence, i.e. her slamming her foot down on his own, and that would have most likely got her kicked out.

With a peek behind, she grinned as she saw the potential buyer had the seller by his collar and had backed him into a bookcase. She could almost see the steam rise from the top of his bald head.

Oh yes, karma was definitely happening.

✝

The glass glistened and sparkled and called to Belinda as she approached the new stall. Her gaze was glued to the tall cabinet that stood to the left of the stall. There were tables and shelves filled with crystal glasses and bowls and even a stand that held just Swarovski crystal. If she hadn't of been so entranced by the perfume bottles, she would have headed for the Swarovski. That was the other thing she loved, there was just something about the sparkling crystal that made her fingers curl in delight.

The seller, a tall man that stood a good two foot above her own height, smiled as she approached. He had grey hair that she could see peek out from under a flat cap and a matching goatee. His eyes were so blue, Belinda was positive that they were contact lenses, as having eyes that shade was surely impossible. He had straight white teeth, which had to be either false or those posh veneers she had seen advertised on the TV. Judgemental, she knew, but she had been around a lot of antiques sellers in her life and as much as they all liked to act like they were the dog's bollocks, the last thing they would sort out would be their teeth.

Belinda frowned and turned a little, pretending to look at a stunning piece of black carnival glass. Why did her mind do this? It chose the most inopportune moments to go off on a tangent about matters that were not important to the moment. She had found that when she was nervous or excited it happened, and had once done it with Mike. Her thoughts had wandered off about the fact his biceps had nearly burst from his overalls when he had been telling her what her car needed. She had missed the entire conversation and had to nod and pretend like she had heard it all. That had been embarrassing, but she had managed to get away with it; she couldn't do that now. Not when there was a possibility that she would buy a new bottle.

She took a long, deep breath then released it just as slow and turned. She smiled brightly when the seller noticed her as she approached the glass case. Every single bottle inside was different and the colours were spectacular and matched nothing she currently owned.

"You like the bottles, yes?" the old gentleman asked, and walked towards her as she stood and stared into the case. His slight accent sounded so exotic, but also friendly and calming

"Yes, yes I do, they are so beautiful," Belinda answered. She smiled briefly at the man before she continued to look at the bottles. One stood out at the back of the case, it was tall and thin, with slight etchings on the glass. It had a subtle blue colour and its small stopper curved in a spiral. Belinda pointed to the bottle.

"Can I see that one please?" she asked, and stepped back to allow the gentleman to access the case, only he didn't move. He just smiled down at her, before he tilted his head to the side.

"You do not want that one." He shook his head and turned on his heel towards his counter. Belinda blinked and stayed where she was. What did he mean, she didn't want that one? Yes, she did.

"Miss, come, I show you something special," the gentleman called out from behind the counter. All she could see of him was his backside as he had bent over at the waist to fetch something from the bottom cupboard. For an older man, he certainly had a nice arse, she thought, as she looked at the said body part cupped in denim. Sweet Jesus. Since when was her mind always in the gutter?

"Here we go," he said, as he stood and placed a small box upon the table before he sat on his stool and waited. His eyes held a hint of excitement and the turquoise almost gleamed. Belinda reached out tentatively to touch the worn wood, but she stopped just short and looked up to the gentleman.

"May I?" she asked. Belinda was not one to touch

any antique without permission. She knew the rule *you break it you buy it,* well, after a few disasters in the past, and she didn't want to make that mistake now.

"Of course, Miss. Touch. Feel. Very special piece indeed, very old as well."

Belinda nodded and her fingertips touched the wood. Inside, her stomach did a flip, she could tell the box itself was old by the wear on the surface, but that meant he would want a small fortune to own this. Slowly, she took the box with both hands and lifted the lid. Regardless of its age, it lifted easily, revealing an interior lined with velvet and there, nestled within, was a small bottle.

Only three inches in height, it shimmered in the light. Its colour was an iridescent purple that changed to pale pinks when moved. It reminded her of the kind of things you would find if you went into the cave of wonders from the film Aladdin. Exotic and tiny. She gently picked the glass up; there was still liquid inside, which would again push the price up, but she knew she didn't care. She cupped it gently in her palm and ran her thumb across the raised words that were scrolled across the centre.

Cupid's Essence

Those simple words pulled at her soul and she had to force herself to put the bottle back into its nest of velvet. She wanted this piece and she knew the gentleman knew it. For some reason he had known she would be interested in something like this.

She wanted to take it home and look at the box and bottle further, take her time to delve into the past and imagine who had owned such a beautiful, mysterious token from the past.

Belinda looked up. "How much?"

She attempted to keep her face devoid of emotion, but she couldn't help the hint of excitement that seemed to bubble up and escape in a huge grin. She waited as the gentleman watched her and once again tilted his head in thought.

"For you, Miss, £500."

Belinda blinked and nearly had to manually close her mouth. "How much?" she answered, her voice squeaking at the end. "I'm sorry, thank you for showing me but I won't be paying that." She pointed once again to the cabinet and back to the blue bottle. "How much is that one?"

"£20," he answered quickly, but made no move to put the one labelled with Cupid's name away, he seemed to watch her carefully and in turn, it made her squirm.

Chapter Seven

Belinda looked from the cabinet with the blue bottle in, back to the counter with the rosewood box. She was truly conflicted, a part of her the moment she had touched the small unique bottle had become attached to it. She wanted it, but she was not prepared to pay £500 for it.

"Why so much?" she asked, "For such a small bottle that's not even made of crystal." She folded her arms and waited for a reply.

"Well Miss, you had best take a seat for this a magical tale."

Belinda fought a battle to stop herself rolling her eyes; now even the gentleman was sounding like he belonged in Aladdin. He nodded towards the spare stool and smiled, it reminded her of one of her old teachers when they were ready to sit for story time, but they could easily blow their fuse if pushed. She unfolded her arms and slid onto the seat and eyed the gentleman warily, she placed her hands into the pockets of her jacket and waited. She wanted to keep her hands out of the way because she had the urge to touch the small, wooden box again, and the bottle that resided within.

"Many years ago Miss, Cupid himself came to earth. He wanted to bring love to the world."

Belinda was struggling to hold back the retort that threatened to burst from her lips. She loved stories like the next girl, but bullshit made up to make her pay the full amount was going to piss her off. He continued on, unaware of Belinda's struggle.

"Cupid wanted everyone to be able to get love and so, he created Cupid's Essence." The gentleman tapped the box, his hand smoothed over the wood, almost like a caress.

"Cupid's Essence was created out of the tears of Cupid, caught into the small bottle the moment he thought he had lost his own love, Psyche. The tears, once collected, were the purest physical form of love and if used correctly, could help the wearer find their heart's desire.

"So…" Belinda stopped him, even though his voice had started to lull her into a sense of calm she hadn't felt in a long time. "You are telling me this bottle right here holds tears from the mythical creature, Cupid?"

"Yes Miss."

"And you expect me to believe that?"

His answer was to shrug but his eyes held a sparkle of humour. Belinda jumped off the stool and pulled her purse from her bag. It was time she tried this haggling lark.

"Ok, I will give you £100 for both bottles, in cash, right now." She smiled and placed five £20 notes on the counter.

The gentleman clutched his heart and looked on in horror. "So little Miss, you wound me. No, £500 for Cupid's bottle and £20 for the other."

Belinda sighed and looked though her purse. The need to own the mythical bottle, whether the story was bullshit or not, had created a pressure in her chest and she knew that annoying twitch of hers would start to kick in soon.

"£150," she countered, she refused to jump in at a high price.

"No," was his only answer. Only this time, he made to put Cupid's bottle back in its box. Belinda panicked.

"£250 for both and that's all I can afford…cash," she breathed out in a rush. That was her purse emptied and would mean no visit to the tea room for cake today, not unless they had started to take card payments within a few hours.

Belinda waited, her heart rate had doubled and she was certain he would say no, his hand hadn't left the box and he eyed her warily.

"You will protect this, Miss? It is no ordinary perfume bottle."

"Of course," Belinda fired back. "My collection is always locked away and taken care of." She felt slightly insulted at his remark, but quickly remembered that he didn't know her and was not aware of her obsessive tendencies that meant her collection was kept in a special room, a shelf for each piece and it was cleaned regular. The lighting was just right, so as not to fade the colours in the pieces and each item was catalogued. Yeah, she had issues, that she knew, but this was who she was.

"I understand, Sir. Does this mean you accept my offer for both bottles?"

"No, the £250 is for Cupid alone."

Belinda went to argue, but a raised eyebrow from the gentleman stopped her before he continued, "The Blue bottle I will gift you for free, a little something for one so beautiful."

Belinda blushed bright red and didn't try to hide it. She spent most of her life hidden away from the world; in her study when she was a student and then in the library as an adult. She had only let others see her as she saw herself; always dressed in her severe uniform. Not as she was now; hair down past her shoulders, simple and light make-up and an outfit that, if she did admit, worked for her.

"Thank you, Sir."

"Please Miss, call me Mr Fati." He smiled as he said this, collected the money from the counter and then proceeded to package up Cupid's essence. She watched as he carefully placed the box that housed the bottle within, in a large velvet bag and then, in turn, wrapped that in a large quantity of bubble wrap. Only then did he collect the other blue bottle from the cabinet and place that within protective packaging.

Belinda watched all this and still her heart rate had not calmed down. She felt she was waiting for that drop on a roller coaster, where they hang you over the edge and then, when you think they won't drop you, they do. It was strange and exhilarating at the same time.

"I will be here next month should you wish to return the bottle, should you find what you need, I will be here."

His words were cryptic but it didn't bother her for

long once she got her hands on the bag containing both bottles. All she could do was smile and repeatedly say thank you before she turned and left the Amor stall.

Still sat in the car thirty minutes later, Belinda couldn't believe she had spent £250 on one bottle all because it said the name 'Cupid' on it. But, hadn't she been hoping for some help in that department? Maybe, just maybe, this would be the turning of the tide for her regarding love. Maybe this small bottle will help her with Mike. What did she have to lose? She had already made a tit of herself. She may as well go the full hog.

Belinda grinned as she turned the engine on. She patted the bag that held her purchases before she pulled off and headed for home. Belinda, unaware of being watched, sang along to the music on the radio as an answering smile flashed across the gentleman's features before he and his stall full of wares slowly vanished, un-noticed by all.

Chapter
Eight

Belinda clutched the bag from the fair to her chest after she had parked the car against the curb, and then walked up the path to her front door. The weather had gone back to being dull and dreary and she couldn't wait to get in and get warm.

She was starving as well. There was still a part of her that was gutted she had spent every bit of cash she had on the bottles and had nothing left for cake. So she had gone home via the supermarket and had picked up a pack of freshly made jam doughnuts. Not that she would eat them all, well, maybe she would but she had to have cake.

Cake was a lot like chocolate; it was the answer to everything.

Pushing the door shut, she walked straight upstairs and then up the second set of stairs to her converted loft. She had converted it not long after she had moved in, finding she didn't have room for all of her books and other collections, and the empty space offered what she needed.

As she walked in she couldn't help but smile, this was her favourite place when she wasn't at work or doing house work. The attic was long and thin, with the stairs coming up half way along. Shelves ran the entire length, on both sides and were filled with her favourite fiction books, reference books and small baskets with her collections of keyrings, magnets, bookmarks and other small random things she thought were cute. One end had been turned into a cosy snug, with a small wood burner, comfy chair with pillows and blankets, small table and a lamp. The brick wall had been draped with thick material to help keep in the heat, along with the insulation that had been installed when the conversion had happened. Where the beams were too low, she had made sure small windows had been installed, not those sky facing windows but the ones that had a windowsill so wide she could place cushions on and watch the world go by.

Conveniently, one had been placed opposite her chair and next to the wood burner. The builder had said it would be a tight squeeze but she didn't care, she could now escape to her room and curl up in her chair, yet still see the outside world and watch it go by. The view looked amazing at any time of the year, especially when the weather decided to create a show. Any time it snowed or a storm rolled in, showcasing its thunder and lightning, she had the best view and could watch with a cup of cocoa.

On the opposite end, built in solid oak with locks that could rival most safes, was her pride and joy. At seven foot high and five feet across, with black smoky shelves, handmade by a local glass worker and lights that had been placed with precision, Belinda owned a stunning piece of furniture that showed off her treasures to the max. Each bottle shimmered under the intense lighting; each one was different, but nothing detracted from their beauty.

It had taken her years to amass the collection, but each one had offered her a chance to meet people and get out of the house. It also taught her that she could use her OCD to her benefit and beat her anxiety. In essence, this was her therapy- well, this and reading.

Next to the elaborate case stood another small table, this in fact matched the one next to her chair. They had beautiful scroll work up the single stand and the tale itself was shiny with age and showed off every grain of the mahogany.

Belinda placed her bag on the top before she reached for her key to the cabinet, hidden in a small niche in one of the beams closest to the unit. She unlocked the glass door using all four keys before turning off the sensors that would trigger an alarm that would wake the whole street. Not that anyone would know about her collection or where it was housed.

She opened the doors and, as was her tradition, she looked at each piece one at a time, remembering the purchases and each story that had accompanied them. She remembered the excitement that had over-taken each and every time, just like it had today, only today felt different somehow. Like this was just the start of a new chapter in her life, which confused her as it was only a couple of bottles. Yes, she had spent more than what she would normally pay but a splurge every now and again wouldn't kill her. Would it?

Carefully, she pulled the blue bottle first from its wrappings and looked it over. It didn't take her long to notice the slight chip in the stopper or the mark-ings across the bottom that would have belonged to a price sticker. As per her routine, she pulled some cleaning materials from the bottom drawer in the cabinet and cleaned off the markings, making it shine; the blues erupting into greens the more she put it in the light.

She placed it on the very top shelf, next to two

other bottles that were similar colours and smiled. She loved how beautiful they looked, it was strange how she wasn't a materialistic person, but owning these treasures made her feel complete.

Finally she reached for the box, her heart once again increased its beats as she pulled the box free from the wrapping until she was left with just the velvet bag. It was, again, strange how she had only seen the box an hour ago, but she couldn't remember what it looked like. It was as if it was a blank in her memory.

Slowly, she removed it from the velvet bag and set it on the table. Her eyes became entranced by the play of light on the glass as she carefully folded the velvet and placed it in the drawer. Now she had the time, she could explore the stunning rosewood box in more detail.

The box itself was around eight inches long, by four inches wide and six inches in depth. Every part was decorated in the small, intricate image of a rose twined with vines and leaves. There was no way to see where they started or ended, even the seal where the box opened could not be determined.

She gently lifted it into her palms and tilted it this way and that, loving the way the light reflected off the wood. It felt so light in her hands and, she leant forward and sniffed, it smelled of summer flowers, teamed with summer rain storms. Though it was only a hint, it made her want to stand and sniff the box harder just to get the smell again.

Belinda placed it down on the table and gently lifted the lid to reveal, once again, the velvet lined interior. The sight of the iridescent bottle caught her breath as she stared at the small glass vial. The liquid left inside swirled, almost like the inside of a lava lamp. She had been sure there had only been a small amount of liquid inside when she had seen it earlier, but now it looked full.

She took the bottle between her fingers and lifted, noting how clear the glasswork was and how this one, unlike the blue one, had zero markings or scratches. The stopper was fixed firmly, she was pleased to note, and the writing looked even clearer now she had it home. The wording of Cupid's Essence was a form of scroll work. How the craftsman had got it into the glass she had no idea, but she would no doubt end up on bloody YouTube, trying to find a video.

The smell of summer rain and flowers hit her nose once again, but this time stronger, the fragrance now emanating from the small bottle. Unable to help herself, she brought it up to her nose and sniffed, this time harder than she had with the box.

As soon as the smell hit her senses, she felt a dizzying rush, her head spun and she had to place a hand against a beam to hold herself upright. Her head felt woozy, but in that pleasant way you get when you've take a painkiller and the pain finally subsides and you feel a tiny bit numb as well as on the edge of consciousness.

Belinda was unable to stop her knees from giving way as she slowly slid down the shelves at her back, until her arse hit the floor. Her fingers, instead of gripping the delicate bottle, relaxed even more and she watched as it slid out of her hand and rolled across the wooden floor. Belinda watched with her heart in her mouth and in slow motion as her body tipped to the side at the same time as the bottle fell. She was positive it would smash, but she felt so light, she almost didn't care. As her head connected with the floor and blackness started to impede on her vision, the bottle also rolled across the floor and instead of smashing into hundreds of pieces, it bounced from the base of the cabinet before it settled near to her, the liquid inside still safe. From her near unconscious mind, the liquid pulsed as if it had a life of its own.

Chapter Nine

Belinda's dreams swirled like a coloured mist. It looked, almost, as if someone had placed small drops of colour in water and then stirred. She felt disorientated and slightly dizzy. Her heart, she could feel, felt like it would pound its way through her chest wall, the thump as her blood pumped through her veins sounded loud and clear in her ears.

This couldn't be a dream, she thought, unable to move or speak, this felt too real. She watched as the colours moved and flowed around her before they took shape.

A woman and a man formed within the colours, dressed in clothing Belinda didn't recognise. The scene expanded, showcasing a large room that shone from thousands of candles that made the ornate furnishings glitter and sparkle. More people became visible, all dressed the same as they danced their way around the room. Music that sounded muffled could be heard and still Belinda couldn't move, only observe.

The ball that took place was stunning to watch and Belinda became entranced watching the couples dance and court, secret glances and looks of lust were thrown. But it was the bent heads of two that held her attention the longest. For some unknown reason, their voices could be heard clearer than anything else in the room.

"Marcella?"

"No Ruben, I have given my answer: no. Please leave it at that."

The lady named Marcella tried to move away from the gentleman but his hand shot out to grab her elbow.

"Marcella," he said through clenched teeth as he stepped closer. "You will agree to this, your father has already given his consent, it will happen."

"What about my consent Ruben, does my opinion on this matter not count at all?"

He laughed but no humour came from it.

"Your opinion has little meaning Marcella, surely you know this."

"You would force me?" She looked into his cold, grey eyes. "Even though I do not love you and never will."

That comment fired his temper and he increased the pressure of his grip on her arm. Belinda could already see the redness of her skin and was sure that once he released her, there would be bruises visible.

"Love means nothing. You have spent far too long gaining the attention of the men at every ball you have attended. That will stop Marcella."

Belinda watched as the lady pulled her elbow from his grip and stood with her chin held high.

"I will not bow to your word Ruben. You may think you can force me, but you will learn I will be forced by no man, especially one as cruel as you." She turned, but not before she glared at him. "You approach me again and I will have you removed. You forget that I may have attracted all the men here tonight, but every one of them would come to my aid if asked. You would do well to remember that a lady does not like to be manhandled. Goodnight."

Belinda watched as the lady, Marcella, moved through the crowd as if nothing had happened. Her eyes bright, she spoke to all with respect and politeness. Her eyes connected with everyone else's, even those that belonged to Ruben. All except for one man that stood off to the side.

He was tall and handsome, broad in the chest and arms. He held himself like a gentleman, but there was a slight wildness in his eyes that made Belinda pause. His own eyes were glued to Marcella and although she never returned his gaze, Belinda knew she was aware of him. The only time he had looked away from her was to shoot glares at the male known as Ruben.

As if pulled, Belinda followed Marcella as she moved to the other side of the room and through the doors to the garden. Once alone, she watched as Marcella found a stone bench surrounded by bushes and as she sank onto it, her shoulders dropped.

"Lord help me," she called out. "I do not know what to do."

Her hand reached into the beautifully beaded purse and pulled out the familiar bottle that Belinda had not long ago held. Marcella's voice held a hint of sadness as she clutched the iridescent glass.

"Before, everything made sense but now, now I'm more confused than ever. I thought you were supposed to help me, not make things worse," she said to the bottle.

"Marcella," a low husky voice whispered through the bush. Belinda caught Marcella's quick movement that hid the bottle in her purse.

"Hello," she answered, her voice wavering slightly. "Who's there?"

The male that had followed her every move stepped from the shadows and Marcella gasped in response. He seemed bigger and his presence made even Belinda grow nervous. But not scared. This man, she could tell, made Marcella nervous in a way that brought a blush to her cheeks. She stood and bowed her head in greeting. Small wisps of her hair fell forward and her dress rustled in the silence.

"Sir."

"My lady," he answered and stepped forward. He took her hand, the one Ruben had been so rough with, and kissed her knuckles. He lingered with his lips on her skin as he waited for her to raise her eyes to meet his. Their eyes met and even Belinda could hear the catch in Marcella's throat.

Belinda felt like an intruder on such a personal moment. But the dream carried on, regardless to her feelings. She felt her own heart continue to thump hard in her chest. She felt a part of her, deep down in her soul, call out for a man to look at her like Marcella was being looked at by this male.

"Can I help you, sir?" She heard Marcella ask, and Belinda felt the butterflies in her own stomach flip as the male smiled.

"I…" he began, his hand still held onto hers, "I have been eager to meet the infamous Lady Marcella, rumours of your beauty have circulated far and wide, but I find them untrue."

Belinda watched as Marcella frowned and tugged her hand free.

"Untrue. Really?" She answered the male. Belinda could swear she could hear the inner workings of Marcella's mind and how this man's opinion of her mattered more than she would dare to admit.

"Yes, my lady, untrue." He walked closer and in turn, Marcella backed up until her back was pressed against the bush she had hidden herself behind. No one knew where she was and they were far enough from the ballroom that if she called out no one would hear her.

"Untrue in the sense that they didn't mention how your hair looks like it was spun from the finest gold. Your eyes are like gems that sparkle in the light and if wanted, they could entrance a man as to forget his own name." He lifted his large, calloused palm and held her cheek.

Belinda watched as Marcella closed her eyes to the touch, entranced by this male's words.

"Your skin is softer than the purest silk, you are a goddess." His last words were a mere whisper, but easily heard.

"Who are you?" Marcella whispered back as her eyes fluttered open.

"Merely a man, smitten by your beauty."

"Will you not tell me your name, so I may know the man that speaks such poetry?" she asked.

"Soon, my lady, meet me here again tomorrow night."

Marcella nodded and closed her eyes as he bent his head. Belinda watched him move from hovering above her lips and instead pressed his own to the spot behind her ear.

"Until tomorrow," he whispered once more and then he was gone, leaving Marcella alone in the night, a smile on her own lips.

Belinda couldn't help but join her in a smile as the colours faded and swirled again before they turned black. Unconsciousness called and she embraced it.

Chapter Ten

Mike hurt everywhere, he didn't think there was one inch of his body that didn't have a bruise, but hell, it had been worth it. His team had won but it had been a battle, and there had been more than a few fights. What good match didn't? But they had come out on top. His only issue now was his hangover from the night before had caught up with him, and that, coupled with the beating on the pitch meant he now felt rougher than a badger's arse.

His head throbbed, his legs ached and his back felt like someone had pressed knives into the flesh. His face would be sporting a bright bruise and the cut under his right eye made it look like he had done a few rounds in the boxing ring, rather than played a great rugby game.

As he slammed the door shut, he let his shoulders sag as tiredness fought to dominate.

The day had given him an unexpected twist. There had been a gypsy fair on, in the field next door to the pitch, and the guys had been bored after the match. A gypsy fair teamed with drunken rugby players didn't exactly match up, but it had worked out as the lads had just got even more leathered on the home brews and Mike… Well, he and found a stall selling remedies to everything from spots to baldness. Lucky for him, he had found one for his stutter. It had cost him £50, but it would be worth it if he could finally talk to Belinda and not sound like a fool.

Dumping his kit on the floor in the kitchen, he collected some painkillers, antiseptic cream and a bottle of water before he headed upstairs to the bedroom. It took him only a few seconds to strip down to his boxers. Mike glanced at himself in the wardrobe mirror as he did and winced at the amount of scratches that could be seen on his back. It was his own fault for not releasing the ball, but the player didn't have to rake on him with such force. His back would become multiple shades of black, blue and purple as the hours progressed.

A hot bath, teamed with the pain killers, would go a long way to making him start to feel human. But he knew he would ache twice as bad the next morning. On his way to the bathroom his foot connected with the charger for his phone and he remembered he had forgotten to take it with him to the match. He unplugged it and took it with him to the bathroom.

Turning on the taps to the bath, he let it run, filling it two thirds full. His size meant if he had it any fuller it would overflow and flood his bathroom. That would cause damage to the downstairs too, and he definitely didn't need that in his life at the moment. It had taken him six years to get the place looking good and the last thing he needed was to trash it.

Mike finished off the bottle of water before he stripped off the tight boxers and climbed into the bath. He groaned with both pain and relief as the hot water went to work on the tired and aching muscles, but also cleaned the scratches and cuts. He placed his head against the lip of the tub and lay there, letting the heat do its thing as he thought about how the day had gone. It didn't take long for his thoughts to drift back to Belinda.

His mate had been right, even if he had denied it; he liked her, a lot. She was so unlike any other woman he had met, and he liked her differences. He liked that she didn't look at him like a piece of meat up for slaughter, but seemed to see him. She had never made fun of his stutter and had always been so friendly. That's why he had left the note. Her rejection did hurt; he would admit that now, here, alone in the bath.

He reached over to the washing basket and plucked his phone from the top. He wasn't surprised to see he had messages from the guys at work- well, messages as in a group chat. They had been talking non-stop, all day, about the ladies they had met the night before and what they had got up to. The word "fucking" had been used to excess, as well as some sordid pictures. Mike wasn't like that, what went down with a lady was his business only. In a sense, he was old fashioned and wasn't really the type of guy that liked to flash a lady's bits around for his mates to see. If she sent a picture, he wouldn't share it around like a pack of biscuits.

He did get a few on nights out, especially when his mates thought it would be funny to hand his number out. Just because he looked the way he did, some women thought he would be open to that sort of thing.

Flicking past the messages and pictures, Mike paused as an unknown number appeared. Clicking onto the message, he read it slowly and blinked. Shit, why did he leave his phone at home?

Shit, shit, shit!

There, clear as day, was a message sent from

Belinda the night before. She had apologised for not replying to his note, and he believed her excuse, as vague as it was. She had always been honest with him and he didn't see her as the kind of girl that would bullshit. She was straight to the point, and that was another thing about her he liked. But he also wondered if beneath that straight-laced exterior was a woman of passion. Her eyes, when he had had chance to look into them, had shown a multitude of emotions, even passion. But it was her spark that drew him in more than anything. She was a puzzle he was eager to solve.

Shit, Mike thought. He once again leaned his head back, his hands lay resting over the rim of the bath tub. He had to think, he couldn't just fire back a smart ass response, he had to take his time and get it right. He read over the message once again.

Mike.

Hi it's Belinda. I wanted to apologise for not messaging you sooner. I have only just found your note in my planner. Please believe me, it wasn't deliberately missed.

I'm so sorry if I have let you down in any way.
Belinda

Opening up a new text he started to type.

Belinda
 Thanks for your message and don't worry about it.
 You fancy meeting for a drink?
 Mike

He pressed send then threw his phone back onto the washing basket before he submerged his head under the water. The cut on his face stung but he stayed under long enough to feel his lungs start to protest. As he came up for air, he pushed his hair from his face, his stubble scratched his palm. He didn't expect an answer straight way but hoped she wouldn't leave it too long. He smiled and thought about where to take her if she agreed to the drink. Did she drink alcohol? There were so many things about her that he didn't know, but he was dying to know everything. He reached out and picked up his bottle of *mint source* body wash and shampoo. Time to clean up and then food, maybe then she will have replied.

Chapter Eleven

Cupid laughed at the TV before he sipped his large fruity cocktail. He had no clue what was in it, he had just raided the drinks cabinet and put a good glug of alcohol from each bottle into the large jug. He had then added some fruit, a dash of orange juice and voila! *Cocktail a la cupid.*

Today had been more entertaining than he had thought it would be, the mortals were more fun in person and he hadn't expected to snare one so easily. The female had been drawn straight to his little makeshift stall, but then again, what female could resist the pull of Cupid? What he didn't expect was for her to resist the pull of Cupid's essence so easily. He may have lied about a few things, but he hadn't lied about what was contained in the bottle.

It did indeed contain the tears he had shed when he had been convinced he had lost his love. He didn't cry, but that time he had been unable to stop the flow of fluid as it had leaked from his eyes. That had made the other gods realise that what he felt had indeed been true love; that Psyche was meant for him, and him alone. They had bottled those tears in an enchanted vessel that would never empty and gifted them to him as an apology for the mistake they had made.

When he had got his lady love back, he had maybe gone a tad "batshit crazy". He grinned, mortal words and phrases always made ranting so much more enjoyable. He had blown his fuse at the other gods and in turn, had made sure they knew what he had gone through times ten. They had quickly begged for his forgiveness, begged for him to lift the curse he had placed on them.

Cupid's annoyingly loud ring tone echoed in the room, Ylvis's high-pitched tone singing *What Does the Fox Say* always made Cupid smile when he heard it. It was the tune he had chosen for his lady love well, because she was his fox. If she knew, he would no doubt get the silent treatment, or a glare, or the familiar birdy. But they always made up and that was worth it. It usually took a few days and left them both spent.

Cupid adjusted himself in his joggers, just the thought of the make up session had him growing hard and it was a waste at the moment. Yes, he was male and loved playing with *Pedro,* but when he had the choice between Psyche's areas of outstanding natural beauty or his hand, he would always go for the national trust option. The sights and sounds were much prettier to look at and he always got cake at the end as well.

"Down boy." He patted his own area of outstanding beauty and reached for his mobile, pleased to see Psyche had obviously been thinking about him whilst she was away. That and she wanted to say thank you for the fabulous dick pic he had sent. What woman could resist that?

Cupid my love-stop playing with it, it will drop off and as much as it has the capability to make me scream I DO NOT want pictures of it. It isn't that pretty.
BEHAVE I will be home soon.
Love
Pxx

Well that wasn't the attitude he was hoping for. Cupid pouted, was he losing his touch? Shit, maybe he needed to be more involved with his current venture, because if he was losing his touch in the love department then he needed to put more effort into it to making sure it worked.

Removing his hand from its comfy position on his cock, he swung his legs around and sat up. The mere thought that he may be losing his immense skills as the god of love was frightening. Or was it just that Psyche was becoming immune? That wasn't on, if so.

Dammit, he needed to be worshiped as the king of lovers, and for her to say *Pedro* wasn't pretty was just rude. In one smooth movement he slid his joggers down his legs and off at his feet. With a confident bounce to his step he walked into the bedroom and to the full length mirror. Yes, he had work to do, but he wanted to show his wife just how pretty *Pedro* was. With his phone in one hand and a bright red bow in the other, he set about a show that would no doubt change her mind and also lead to some special tours of his favourite valleys.

Cupid grinned as he tied a bow.

Oh yes, she would be helpless to resist.

†

Belinda groaned as she opened her eyes. Gently, she rolled over from her horizontal position on the floor of her loft. Her brain was fuzzy and she felt like she had swallowed moth balls.

What the hell had happened? She almost never fainted and she had never in her life passed out like that before. She remembered taking a deep whiff of the perfume in her new bottle and feeling out of sorts. Belinda looked around the floor but was unable to see the bottle. Despite her state, she crawled along the floor, looking underneath all of her bookcases in her search. She hope she hadn't smashed it, there was a lot of money tied up in the small glass bottle and regardless of the fact she was a little spooked by it now, she couldn't just afford for it to be in pieces on the floor.

Using the closest case to help her stand, she brushed the dust from her clothes and looked at her watch.

"Shit," she blurted out. The time was 5:48am. Belinda had been out for the count for hours, no wonder she felt like she had spent the night on a rack. She groaned again as she twisted in an effort to stretch her muscles. She stopped mid twist as her eyes fell on her display case. She was positive that she had left it open, ready to place the bottle inside, but now there it was on display, as if the night's event had never happened. The rosewood box was open and showed the small bottle nestled inside the velvet. There was something different, but Belinda couldn't quite put her finger on it.

She again couldn't take her eyes off it as it shimmered and almost pulsed. She shook her head and turned away from it. This was the freakiest night she had ever had.

"Maybe I should take it back?" She looked over her shoulder as she said the words and her eyes widened as the liquid inside the bottle pulsed stronger and changed colour- to red.

Mesmerised, she opened the case that hadn't been locked and reached in to grab the pulsing bottle. In her hands, it vibrated slightly as if angry at the threat to return it.

"I'm sorry," she said, feeling like a muppet for talking to a bloody bottle. "I won't return you if you don't want me to." She watched as the angry, red colour slowly faded back to the pink she remembered from before. The vibration calmed to a slight buzz and the bottle felt warm in her hand.

Belinda was stunned at the reaction. She smiled and asked another question. "Are you going to help me?"

The answer was instant, the bottle buzzed harder and the colours started to include blues and purples.

The smell that she adored filled the room. She breathed deep and smiled more brightly.

"Thank you, whatever you are." It buzzed again, but when she went to return it to the box in the display case it vibrated violently, showing its dislike for being in the case.

"You don't want to be in the case then?"

It vibrated in answer and Belinda chuckled. "You are a stubborn thing, aren't you? Come on, you and the box can live in my room." She picked up the box from the case and slid the bottle back into his velvet home before she locked the case. She made her way down the stairs, turning off the lights as she went. Her feet were silent on the carpet as she walked into her bedroom and placed the box on her dressing table. Her fingers slid over the wood in an almost caressing way. Each pattern that had been etched onto the wood called for her fingers to explore it. She was almost ready to sit down and do that when she remembered what time it was and where she had spent the night. She felt icky and in need of a shower. Belinda, with an absent mind, patted the box and walked towards her bathroom.

She didn't just feel icky, but not entirely herself. Her skin felt tingly and her stomach felt like it was full of butterflies. Undressing and dumping her clothes onto the floor, she stepped into the shower and turned on the water full tilt. The spray, at first, was cold and made Belinda scream, as well as making sure she was truly awake before it warmed. The water streamed down and onto Belinda's face as the steam filled the room. Nothing felt as good as the feeling of hot water running down her naked body. She would assume the touch of a man equalled that but, she didn't know. Hell, she had only been kissed the once. Belinda shuddered under the spray at the thought.

Memories, again of her turbulent childhood, filled the current void in her mind, bringing back the feelings of not fitting in and being on her own. Her parents had always done the best for her, but with her issues she struggled to fit in. You had the usual taunts of; swot, miss goody two shoes and others. She couldn't help that when she focused on her school work it helped take her mind from going into over-load about things that she couldn't control. Like the dust in the classroom, or the books not being in alphabetical order, the colours of the pencils not neatly arranged. The list could go on and on. Her teachers hadn't noticed both the taunts and the issues she had, and Belinda hadn't wanted to tell her parents, so that was when she had started relying on herself.

As she got older, the taunts became more hurtful and she was called more names because she was never interested in boys and kept to herself. She had been labelled a lesbian by the shallow minded lads of her school for this fact. She did despair when lads treated girls like that and then had the nerve to wonder why they found it hard to get a girlfriend. When she was that age, it seemed to be the only thing that mattered for her classmates. Well, not for her, she had learned early on that maturity took a while, especially when the owner had a penis, so she kept clear.

Belinda sighed and bent her head forward so the water could flow down her back. The warmth seeped into her muscles, relaxing the knots that had been formed from her night on the floor. Her mind swirled and once again focused on Mike.

Now, he wasn't the type of guy most people would assume she would go for; they expected her to be married to a professor or another academic. Why, she had no idea, the mere thought of that bored her to the max. Why she needed someone like that when she did that herself was baffling. She wanted someone that would push her out of her comfort zone, break the mould that she had been set in for so many years and if she followed the way her heart wanted, it pointed straight to Mike.

There was something about his large muscles that spoke to her of protection and safety, along with his gorgeous eyes that she wanted to sink into. Yes, he was your typically good looking guy, but he had a vulnerability that called to her. His stutter wasn't annoying, it actually was endearing to her and she loved listening to his voice, so the longer he took the better.

She sighed again, this time louder. Her body feeling tired and relaxed, she turned off the water and picked up a towel. Her body felt almost limp, she had become suddenly exhausted as she wrapped herself in the soft material and walked back into her room.

She missed the text that lit her phone and she missed the box as it vibrated on her dressing table, the lid now open and the bottle pulsing with a strange purple light.

All she cared about was getting under the covers of her soft bed and sleeping. Pulling the duvet back, she climbed in and snuggled down, her mind shutting down and sending her once again to sweet oblivion, even as Cupid's Essence worked its magic.

✝

Cupid's magic flowed and surged from his fingers

as he picked up on the bottles presence. No mortal could see him, which was handy considering he was still dressed in those jogging bottoms he favoured and had no shirt on. If they could see, both males and females would flock to be near him-yes, he was that irresistible and sexy and hot. The list would go on, if he had the time.

He didn't feel the cold, which again, was lucky, but he also couldn't linger in the cold, half dressed and flexing his fingers like Mr Tickle in attack mode. His magic, although it was his, could and would be felt by the other immortals if he used too much in a short space of time. This meant the chance of getting busted by his wife got higher and higher the longer he stayed.

Not that he would have minded. Usually, getting busted equalled a make up session, but after the response to his specially crafted photo message with red bow, she was now subject to Cupid's silent treatment, and he had decided she didn't deserve any of *Pedro* for a while. Yes, he would put his wife on a sex ban.

Cupid tilted his head to look up at the house he had aimed his magical touch at and frowned. Did he really just say that in his head?

"Sex ban? Really?" he said out loud as his fingers

continued to do their thing. Only an immortal could see the strings of magic that flowed and surged into the house.

Keeping one hand up and working, Cupid pulled the waist band on his joggers so he could see into them and look at his own man dangle.

"Sorry Pedro, I did say sex ban and it's for our own good." He nodded and smiled sadly. "She needs to learn to appreciate us again." He then let go of his joggers and patted his bulge. All the while, his other hand kept with the finger flexing.

"Lady, you better appreciate getting the personal Cupid treatment," he grumbled. His hands lowered and he sighed. "Coz if you don't get your love life sorted then it means I've lost my mojo and well, that cant fucking happen." In a childlike act, he stamped his foot.

"I'm Cupid for fuck sake, god of love, lord of romance, fucking sexy bastard and I will not lose my mojo because I like getting spanked by the missus!" He stopped and blinked, then whispered in a very Hagrid like way, "Maybe shouldn't have said that."

Head bent, Cupid turned away from the house that now sported a bright pink heart above the roof. Only the most sensitive to magic would get a mild glimpse of it. The dawn was quiet as he walked away.

His bare chest glistened in the rising sun as he turned up the street.

"And no, I'm not gay. I have a wife, duh!" he mumbled to his groin. "I just like pink! Pedro, I thought you were on my side?"

Cupid needed a time out, with tequila.

Chapter Twelve

Belinda blinked slowly as she returned from the land of nod and made it back to the land of the living. She felt strangely calm and, oddly enough, not tired at all. In fact, she felt the most refreshed she had ever done. Usually she wasn't really a morning person and it, on average, took a good hour for her to be awake and human enough to function.

Most mornings consisted of her alarm going off about three times until she would crawl out of bed and into the shower. After that it would take a strong cup of tea and then she would get dressed. By this point, she would have been up for just over an hour and nearly ready to face the world. But now, Belinda frowned up at the ceiling, now she felt like she could bounce out of bed and take on the world.

She turned her head to look at her clock and smiled when she saw it was only 5:30. She chuckled, she had only slept the day away so no wonder she felt so refreshed. Reaching over to her bedside table, she picked up her mobile phone, only to nearly drop it.

It wasn't 5:30pm it was 5:30am, on Monday morning. She had managed to sleep away a whole day and night. Belinda sat up in bed and turned on the light of her small lamp. She noticed she had received a text but she ignored it for the time being. Things didn't feel right. Yes, she felt refreshed and awake but she didn't feel herself. Climbing out of bed, she headed for the bathroom, only to stop in front of her full length mirror by the door.

Belinda tilted her head as she looked at herself dressed in black PJ bottoms and a lacy vest. Strange, she thought, she was positive she had gone to bed in just the towel she had used from the shower. Her hair hung loose and was somehow way past her shoulders, when it had only just reached her shoulders before, it looked shinier than usual and slightly wavy. She loved how it looked but its sudden growth confused her, that and the fact her skin looked clear and almost rosy, her eyes were bright and also clear. She leaned in closer to look; she shook her head, convinced she had seen a tinge of pink around her irises.

When she stepped back she looked again at her entire reflection. She looked good, not that she looked bad before, but everything just seemed fuller and well, positive. Well that didn't make sense, Belinda thought, and then moved away to get ready for the day. It didn't matter, she would just put it all down to a bloody good day and night's sleep and get on with her week.

She paused at her wardrobe and looked over the rails, most of her clothes were dark in colour as that was what she preferred but today she felt she needed a little colour. Her eyes snagged on a splash of red that was hidden on the far side of the rail. She pulled it out and smiled. Perfect.

†

Belinda sipped from her large mug of tea and she looked out over her back garden as she sat at her small breakfast table. The unusual feeling of being ready to take on the world still hadn't gone and it was now two hours later. She was now dressed in a vintage style red dress and she had, for the first time in years, left her hair down and she didn't feel as uncomfortable as she first thought she would.

Belinda had, of course, taken the bottle out of the box once again and had even ventured this time as to remove the stopper and smell the contents directly. There was something about the scent that called to her and before she could stop herself, she had dabbed the perfume on her pulse points before she placed it back inside the ornate box and then picked it up and took it with her to place in her hand bag. Why she needed to take it with her she had no idea, but it was as if she had no control on what she did with the bottle. She would think it and then next moment she was already half way through doing the action.

Her logical, OCD side should be flipping its shit but she found she was too relaxed at the moment. She heard the bottle vibrate in her bag. She smiled and picked her bag up as well as her coat; also a bright red that matched the dress.

"Come on then, let's go to work." She spoke to her bag as if it was the most normal thing in the world as she pulled on her coat and walked to the door. "Let's see what fun we can have."

There was that tiny part of Belinda that was on edge and confused by how she suddenly looked and how she acted. Both were out of her normal comfort zone and not at all her character. That side was soon shushed by the other side of Belinda that, in essence, wanted to live life to the full.

She felt almost torn, like two sides were tugging and fighting for dominance and at the moment, the playful, I don't give a shit side was winning. Belinda breathed deep, catching the scent of her new perfume that blended with her own smell perfectly. Instantly it gave her a buzz and had her hopping out the door. As per usual she looked to her left in the hopes of seeing Mike, but there looked to be no sign of him. Pity, she thought, she was in the perfect frame of mind to ask him out.

Even though the temperature had dropped again to close to zero, Belinda felt warm enough in just her coat. She smiled as she locked the door and practically bounced down the steps to her car. Another look in the direction of Mike's house made her frown, but that was soon forgotten as she climbed in and started the engine. It revved a little before she slid it into gear and started her drive to work.

✝

Belinda looked at the clock above the door in her office; lunch time. She grinned and for once, she was starving. Instead of her usual sandwich in her bright purple lunch box, she had instead opted to have lunch delivered from the café down the road. So as soon as the time had been reasonable- yes, she had been over an hour early for work- she had called and ordered a hot lunch. Daft, but it was something she rarely got and would no doubt feel the need to nap afterwards, but she was looking forward to it.

Her morning had been surprisingly good. She had initially thought it was going to be a complete disaster when she was rudely cut up on a roundabout, she had, of course, used the horn and much to her displeasure, the culprit had circled the roundabout only to come after her and follow her all the way to where she parked for the day.

She had been ready for an argument, but that had never happened. The driver of the other car had parked a few spaces away and when she had collected her bag and stepped out of the car, he had revealed himself.

The driver of the Audi had been a good looking guy with dark hair and brown eyes. He had smiled, almost embarrassed as he got out of his own car to walk across to her. He had been dressed in a suit and had obviously been on his way to whatever he did for a living.

Before she had been allowed to say anything about him cutting her up, he had started to apologise profusely. She hadn't been able to answer him as he had spoken about how angry he was and he had followed in the hopes of stopping and giving the driver a piece of his mind. Belinda had been very tempted to point out that the near on collision had been his fault, but he never gave her chance. Instead, he had then gone on to speak about how once he had parked the car he had watched as she had got out of her own and was overcome by how stunning she was.

Belinda had then been speechless, she had never had a guy openly say something so bold and the more he spoke, the more she found she was unable to answer. He had finished the one sided conversation by handing her his business card and then he had bent and kissed her cheek before hopping into his car and driving away, but not before he waved in a cute school boy way.

As expected, she had stood in the car park and had just looked at the business card for a good five minutes before she had moved and headed to work. She was still surprised hours later as she waited on her lunch to arrive.

She grinned wide when the small door alarm sounded to signal someone entering the library. Belinda stood, purse in hand, and a smile on her face. The delivery guy was good looking and would be the second surprise of the day.

He placed her lunch on the counter and just smiled back, making Belinda squirm a little. He was tall- well, taller than her and had long, blonde hair that was tied back into a small pony tail. Belinda usually didn't think men suited long hair but this blue eyed stranger seemed to pull it off.

"Hi," he said in a very low voice that made Belinda's stomach flip.

"Hi," she replied, very aware of his presence as he leaned on the counter and stared. Belinda looked at him then looked down at her purse, suddenly feeling a little shy.

"How much do I owe you?" she managed to say, although it was quiet.

"For you, gorgeous? Just a kiss and it's all yours." He grinned as he said it. Belinda flicked her eyes up to look at him again, he was still staring but this time he was taking a look at more than Belinda's face. She felt herself blush bright red and jerkily thrust a £10 note in his direction.

"Here you go," she blurted out. He answered with a smile.

"You got a pen?" His voice seemed to be lower and his eyes had darkened.

"Err, yeah sure," Belinda answered and held out the pen. Only for him to grab the hand it was in and tug her forward. He leaned further over the desk and pressed his lips to hers in the first kiss she had received in over six years and for the second time that day, Belinda stood still in shock.

His lips felt so soft against her own and ended sooner then she ideally would have liked. On any other day she would have smacked the stupid grin off his face just for grabbing her hand, never mind kissing her. But today she just smiled shyly and watched as he pulled back, only to use the pen to write something on her palm.

With one last grin in her direction he started to head back towards the door, calling out as he left.

"Lunch is on me, sweetness. Call me."

She stood and stared at the door again for a good five minutes after he had left, unable to process what had happened. In the space of the morning she had been approached by two random strangers. She looked down at her hand to see a name and number written, and they had given her their numbers. What the ever loving hell is going on?

Surely this wasn't normal. She had spent so long being the one that was over looked and all of a sudden, boom, two in one day. She laughed at the craziness of it all. Belinda pulled her lunch from the counter and flopped down into her chair. Her appetite had vanished, although the food that had only cost her a kiss smelt good. But she didn't feel like eating. She felt giddy and flushed and she loved it.

Was this what the trio had been talking about when they had spoken about the joys of being young and experiencing life as well as love? Now she had sort of experienced it, she was keen for more.

Belinda pulled her planner from her bag and placed the business card from Carl, aka, Audi driver in and also wrote down the number from Pete, aka, delivery man down. She would decide whether to contact them or not when she was at home.

The ringing of the phone pulled Belinda's attention back to her job and away from the events of the morning. She did, after all, have a lot to get done before she could finish later on. Unfortunately, she had let things distract her, which wasn't like her at all. She definitely didn't feel like herself, she thought, as she headed back into the office to answer the call, completely unaware of the bottle vibrating happily in her bag.

✝

Belinda walked into her house and only made it as far as the kitchen before she slumped into the chair at the table. What a bloody day, she thought. There had to be something in the air. The morning had been great with the impromptu kiss, but as the day had gone on the library had gotten busier than usual.

At first she had thought nothing of it, but every single visitor had been a man and nearly every single one had come up to the desk to ask the most bizarre questions.

Where are the books on love?

Karma sutra, do you have it in?

Books on romance please?

Then things had changed, she had been asked over ten times for her number and had more than that leave her little notes. They had all smiled sweetly at her like she was the first woman they had ever seen, and it had caused hairs to stand up on her neck. That wasn't normal, There was only one answer and that was Cupid's Essence.

All of this strangeness had started when she had first opened the damn box, and then after she had sniffed it. Belinda sat with her head in her hands as she mulled over and the events that had occurred since she had acquired the bottle. The constant vibrating of the bottle in its box pulled her attention to her handbag.

With a sigh she pulled it from her bag and placed it on the table. The shimmering light that usually accompanied the vibration couldn't be seen as the box was shut. She pulled it closer and this time, instead of going straight for the contents, she looked at the detail in the wood. The bottle seemed happy with the attention, stopped its vibrating and stayed silent, only the pulsing of the colours continued.

The wood detail was stunning, but what drew her attention was the section at the back that held detailing that was completely different to the rest. The area wasn't very big but instead of roses… instead it was swirling letters that spelled out the word, Amour. She gently swept her thumb over the section, feeling each indentation in the wood.

Why was this bit different?

She pressed a little harder on the section and smiled as a small click sounded and the section slid out of the base of the box. Inside, neatly tucked into the crevice, was a scrap of parchment, yellowed with age and a small leather diary. For not the first time since she had had possession of the box and contents, her heart rate picked up, this time with excitement. Placing the diary to the side, she picked up the parchment and carefully unfolded it, laying it flat upon the table.

Neat, elaborate writing flowed across the page and

it took a moment for Belinda to recognise the language.

"French, it's in French," she said out loud, then once again bent her head. There were only a few words she could make out. Wanting to find out what the parchment said, she picked it up, along with the box and diary, and headed towards the lounge and her laptop. She hoped Google could help, otherwise she would have find someone that spoke French.

Please be warned

Cupid's Essence is not what you think.

I warn you now, do not think lightly of this magical item. I happened upon it by chance.

Cupid created this, please believe me. It was made with the sole purpose to help find love.

It has done that, I agree, but it does so much more. But please be on your guard.

Choose wisely, for it has a mind of its own and it is not afraid to meddle, and it surely will.

Use it lightly I beg, the god means well but...

I must go...I pray love finds you.

Be well

Lady Marcella Rousseau

Chapter Thirteen

Still no text, Mike frowned and stuffed his phone back into the pocket of his overalls. She obviously didn't want to go for that drink then. He looked out of the garage window of his house, towards that of Belinda's and was tempted to go over and talk to her, but he knew he wouldn't be able to get a decent sentence out if he did. His stutter always got worse when he tried to talk to Belinda and made him feel inferior and like he was back at school.

That was a feeling he hated, school had been hard with a stutter and it had only been his size and muscle that had prevented him from being picked on. But he had seemed to grow out of it until it came to women. He was lucky in the sense that some only needed a smile and a nod, but he didn't want that anymore. He was getting older and as such, he wanted to finally be able to settle down.

So why was he finding it so damn hard?

Maybe it was time he tried the tonic he had

bought, that would be something he would do later on. What would it hurt to try? If it worked well, then that would be a bonus, but maybe he should just get a grip and deal already.

He was stuck on Belinda. That was the long and the short of it. But he didn't know what to do to get her to see him for more than the mechanic she thought he was. He could offer her so much, if only she would give him the chance. How did he say that to her without sounding desperate, as well as a pussy?

He headed upstairs and made quick work of getting changed and showering, he wanted to head straight back out before he lost his nerve. She would be home, that he knew, so he would go round and knock on and try to ask her out in person.

What would he say? He rolled his eyes and would have bitch slapped himself upside of the head if he could. That had to have been the daftest question yet.

"Fuck. Fuck. Fuck," he mumbled to himself as he stood under the spray and made quick work of washing the day's grease and oil from his body. It always surprised him how much crap came out of his hair and off his skin after a day in the garage. The water, at first, ran an oily brown but soon cleared and he soaped up within an inch of his life.

He loved the feeling of the hot water as it sluiced down his body, easing any leftover aches from his weekend match. Most nights he would have a long soak in the tub, his fellow players knew he had a fondness for a good quality bubble bath and they would take the piss out of him for it by buying him bottles of bubble bath. Mike wasn't worried, he would get them back on the playing field at training. It always made him laugh to see them give him a wide berth. But regardless of how long it took, he would always get even.

Tonight Mike felt on edge, he had felt it all day if he was honest, and the need to see Belinda had been extremely hard to resist. Usually, once he was engrossed in his work he wouldn't really think of anything, but today had been different. He hadn't been able to focus at all and had even nearly fucked up a clutch change.

All he kept seeing in his mind's eye was her beautiful face and her stunning smile that lit her up and made her glow brightly.

Jesus Christ, he thought as he turned the water off and got out, not bothering to wrap the towel around him, instead he started to mop up the water as he walked. There was something going on, something that had him rushing to get ready and making him believe it was urgent he go round to see her.

Mike, not sure what else to think, got dressed before he walked down the stairs and picked up his keys before he headed straight out of the door. Now he would see if he had the bollocks to go through with it.

✝

Belinda's doorbell rang and pulled her from Google it had been a hard couple of painstaking hours, Belinda had finally written out the letter in what she hoped was the correct translation. With a lingering look, she turned and headed for her front door, not sure who it would be.

She hadn't changed since she had got home from work and she knew she didn't look her best.

Opening the door, she stared.

"Mike...err, hi."

He didn't speak, only nodded. He was again dressed in jeans and a jumper, but what stood out stark was the bruising and cut on his face.

"Shit Mike, are you ok, what happened?"

He just smiled then shrugged before he finally started to talk.

"Hey...th-th-this is noth-nothing," he laughed. "The oth-other guy wa-was worse."

"Other guy? What the hell have you been doing?"

Belinda stepped forward and put her palm to his cheek. She continued to check his face even though he had frozen and was watching her.

"Ru-Rugby game," he said, and it took Belinda a few seconds to twig what he was saying.

"Ooh right, got you." She realised what she was doing and stepped back, and before she had chance to stop herself she blurted back, "You don't speak or read French by any chance, do you?"

He didn't answer for a good few long seconds; instead he tilted his head with a small smile before he nodded gently.

"You do?" she said excitedly and waited for the second nod; that was something she had never expected. As it came, she grabbed his arm and tugged him into her house, she closed the door and ushered him into the living room.

"You aren't messing me about are you Mike, about speaking French?"

He smiled again as he sat down on her small sofa, his sheer size dwarfed it. He looked about her small living room before he looked back her and once again nodded.

"Ye-Yes, I speak Fre-French."

She just stood and looked down at him. How did a guy built like a brick shit house and with the looks that could make panties drop, know French?

Well why the hell not, it was narrow minded of her to think otherwise.

"Wow, I'm impressed Mike, when did you learn?"

He shrugged again, making little of an impressive talent. There definitely weren't many men like him that could speak many languages.

"France," he said without a stutter. "I pla-played rug-rugby there."

"Wow, that's amazing," she fired back, impressed even more. "Shit, I'm sorry, where are my manners. Can I get you a drink?" she asked- well, more along the lines of blurted it out.

She smiled as he laughed in response, before he shook his head.

"No-No thank you, I'm go-good."

She nodded but still left the room. One, so she could get her breath and two, she needed a drink. He was in her home, sat on her sofa and her heart was pounding so loud she was convinced he would be able to hear it. So now she had him here what would she do with him?

She shook her head and as she stood in front of the fridge, she leaned her forehead against the door. This was the part where she actually did regret her choice to stay a virgin, because if she wasn't, then she clearly wouldn't be stood in the kitchen needing Dutch courage. Instead, she would have pounced on him and taken advantage. She had plenty of ideas after watching quite a few porn movies.

"Be-Belinda, yo-you ok?" his calm, deep voice sounded from the lounge, so she quickly opened the fridge and grabbed the bottle of fruit cider that had been in there for what had to have been a few months. She quickly opened it and drained some of the contents and swiped the back of her hand across her lips. What the hell was wrong with her?

"Yes I'm fine, I will be right there."

She didn't do shit like this…ever.

Trying to act calm, she walked back into the front room, without the cider, and sat on the sofa next to Mike. She felt drawn to his side, she could have sat anywhere, but instead chose the seat right next to him.

He smiled as she sat and all Belinda could do was return the smile. She felt like she had started to heat up from the inside, she was edgy, almost irritable. She couldn't stop her hands that twisted the sleeve of her top as she avoided looking in Mike's direction.

His large body moved ever so slightly before she felt hands on her own, she watched as they engulfed them and stopped them from tugging. His breath whispered across her cheek before she heard his un-stuttered words in her ear.

"Stop Bel, stop and look at me."

His voice pulled at her insides, the butterflies morphed into something much bigger and she was helpless to resist his command. She turned her head slightly and looked straight into eyes that mirrored her own confusion and obvious desire. His own flicked down to her lips and then back up to her face before a hand slid behind her head, gently fisting her hair as his lips descended upon her own.

She should stop this, they had barely spoken a full sentence to each other, yet, this felt right, it felt perfect. So Belinda closed her eyes the moment the soft skin of his lips touched hers.

He coaxed and caressed, taking his time to explore before his tongue swept across her full lower lip in a bid for her to open and grant him access. Belinda went with it; she opened and became lost in the taste that was Mike. His hand tightened on her hair and she lost the battle to keep a groan to herself.

It surprised her as she felt swept up in a tide of want and need. Somehow her own hands now gripped his large biceps as she hung on throughout the kiss. He awakened every sense, made her feel more than she ever had. Her OCD had been sated by his near presence and now she felt like she wouldn't be able to stay in her skin.

Belinda let Mike lean her back on the sofa. She loved the feel of him as he hovered above her. His size and strength never scared her, only made her feel protected and cherished and the way he continued to kiss her, she would be willing to bare even her soul to him.

Mike didn't rush the kiss, even when they were horizontal on the sofa he kept the pace slow, as if savouring every movement, every touch. Belinda was lost and for once her mind had no control, she let her body lead the way.

"Belinda." She heard him breathe her name as he kissed along her jaw line, this act boosting the butterfly effect in her stomach and pushing her towards neediness.

"Mike," she answered. He pulled back and his hands pushed strands of hair from her cheeks as he looked into her eyes, a small smile on his lips.

"You are so beautiful," he said, and this time with

almost no stutter. His voice deep, he continued to stroke the skin of her cheek before he moved his thumb over her bottom lip.

"Yo-You have no-no idea how long I've wai-waited to kis-kiss you."

Belinda blushed then smiled back, but didn't answer; she didn't know what to say. What did a girl say when a guy says some deep and meaningful stuff like that whilst he's got you flat on your back on the sofa?

Belinda has always classed herself as weird and random so when she opened her mouth she wasn't surprised by what flew out. What she had been thinking at the back of her mind and didn't actually want to say, well not at this precise moment.

So instead of stating how she was over the damn moon to finally be in his arms or something to the same soppy effect, she blurted out, "Nice, would you take a look at something for me, you know to make sure ive translated it right from French to English?"

If she could have smacked her head with her hand she would have, and the total confusion on Mike's face said how much of a total screw up she was.

"Err su-sure." He slowly pushed himself up and off her and helped her to sit upright. He smiled again, but this time it didn't reach his eyes. She had once again stuck her foot in it. Head bowed, she stood up and made an attempt at smoothing her hair and clothing before she walked over to her small desk and picked up the small piece of paper that had the French note on.

Chapter
Fourteen

The dream that assaulted Belinda that night was different from the previous strange swirl of colours she had had. This time there was no pre-empting or warning, nope, they went straight into a scene she had never in her life witnessed before.

At first the sun shone so brightly it had taken a few minutes for Belinda to see, but once she did, she was faced with one of the many wonders of the world.

The great pyramids of Giza filled the vista, along with the glistening Nile and greenery from the river's side. Directly in front, though, stood a temple bright with colours and statues, people milled about dressed in what she assumed Egyptians wore. She had no idea really.

A procession approached and Belinda was transfixed at the wealth on show. A team of servants or slaves carried a platform on which was the most beautiful woman Belinda had ever seen.

Dressed in gold- no not dressed, more like coated in gold- she sat, chin held high, back straight on her mobile throne. One name races through Belinda's head as her dream feet followed the procession.

Cleopatra!

This was the famous queen of Egypt, this was the woman that supposedly brought the Roman Empire to its knees for a short period of time.

Belinda snorted to herself as she kept pace with the procession. It felt strange to be witnessing all of the splendour and also know she was dreaming. But wasn't that the myth of Cleo? She seduced the Caeser, then cheated on him with his general and then when she got found out she killed herself rather than be put on trial. That's what some of the history books had said. But, then again, who could trust those same history books. Most had been written by men and most would believe that Cleopatra had deserved her fate.

The whole situation had sounded completely fucked up to Belinda and if she was honest she had little sympathy for the queen. If she was going to sell her wares to more than one buyer then she should have been prepared for the consequences. But another part of her wanted to know the truth, the unblemished truth of a woman who showed power and strength, equalling that of any man.

The dream was so realistic that Belinda very nearly walked into someone and only dived to the side at the last minute. She felt for the slaves that had to carry the platform, she could see their muscles bulging under the strain. As Belinda managed to catch up, she stepped up onto a wall so she was at an equal height to the platform; it was only then she saw a familiar item.

No box could be seen, but the bottle that held Cupid's Essence sat on a small cushion to the left of the queen. Its colours pulsed and swirled, the familiar pinks and purples called out to her and had her fingers clenching in a bid to touch it.

The procession stopped as local people started to assemble. Belinda could only watch as men of all ages fought to get closer to the queen and as the wind picked up, she recognised the scent that wafted her way.

Summer rain.

Cleopatra was wearing the essence and as Belinda breathed in more of the delicious scent, she realised the queen was drenched in it.

The men became more and more forceful as they reached and grabbed. Whatever the essence was, it called to the men. She had been witness to it herself that very day, but the why's still confused her.

She had assumed it was an ordinary perfume, but now she doubted it was merely that.

Ever since she had brought it home, things stranger than anything she had dealt with before had happened. The mob of what could only be described as horny men became more and more violent.

Belinda could do nothing but watch as guards entered the fray in a bid to rescue the queen and there, amongst the males, one dressed in the armour of the Roman Empire appeared and battled his way through to the platform. She watched, transfixed, as he jumped upon the platform that was still being held by all the slaves and wrapped his arms around the queen. There was no false love in his eyes; he showed only courage, love and determination to get his woman.

As Belinda's dream started to waver back into colours, her last thought was,

why didn't the slaves drop the damn platform?

Chapter Fifteen

Cupid sat perched on a bookcase in the library, his legs swinging as he watched the show below. His chosen mortal, she worked hard below trying to keep up on her jobs, all the while dealing with the influx of men that seemed to be constantly coming into the library.

They used the excuse of checking out a book to check her out. He was impressed she had dealt with them all like the classy lady she was, but he could now see the strain as she managed to turn number twelve around and send him back out into the world with little more than hope that she would call him with the number he had forced into her hand when he had grabbed it to kiss her knuckles.

This was the Essence's doing and Cupid was impressed by how quick and how potent it was. Usually in other cases… Cupid quickly pushed those memories from his mind. It didn't do well to dwell on the past.

Poor Belinda, he thought, it must be exhausting being lusted after.

"Naaa," he said. "She's loving every moment of it."

Talking to himself had become a habit since his wife had buggered off on a silly ladies holiday. Luckily, no one could hear his personal ramblings as he had done a Harry Potter and donned his invisibility cloak. The only difference was Cupid looked sexy as fuck and he did an altogether different style of wand play.

As much as he loved people watching, he was getting bored, but it just so happened he was perched on the top of the classical mythology section.

With a grin he wriggled onto the tall ladder and started his search, slowly perusing the titles on show before collecting a handful.

He paused halfway down the ladder and looked over his shoulder to the mortal, expecting her to be looking at him as he hadn't been quiet and the site of floating books would shit anyone up. She couldn't hear him as he talked complete crap to himself, but as he said, he hadn't been quiet whilst he was grabbing the books. He smirked as he looked at the few that had been dropped to the floor. Nope, she had her head bent doing whatever librarians did.

Other than put books away, what did they do?

He tilted his head and frowned then continued down the ladder with the pile of books balanced on top of each other in his hand.

Dumping the load on the first table he arrived at, he was happy it was sort of hidden but he could still see her bent head. He wasn't bothered if anyone saw his floating trick or if the mortal questioned how a big pile of books had moved. He was Cupid and he did what the fuck he liked… within reason… if the wife allowed it.

With a shake of the head to dispel any negative thoughts of being under the thumb, he picked up the biggest one titled "Myths and legends" and started to thumb through it for the pictures. He couldn't be arsed with words, he wanted to see his sexy self in these books and then maybe he would read what an amazing and awesome god he was. Only the first picture caused him to stop, his voice slightly stunned.

"What the fuck a doodle do!"

He bent closer to inspect the picture, still not able to believe what his own eyes were witnessing. There was a detailed copy of a painting of what these mortals thought he looked like, under it a caption that said 'The fable of love'.

"That is not what I look like, what the holy fuck!"

he shouted. "I do not wear nappies, nor do I have fucking wings and what in the name of Pedro's dangle is that fucking bow?"

He was stunned as shit. Since when did his legend and legacy dictate he be a small sodding cherub that flew around and shot arrows into people's backsides?

If he wanted to poke someone in the arse it would be his wife, and it wouldn't be a fucking arrow at that.

Cupid slumped into a nearby chair, is that why no one believed anymore? Because of this? He pushed away the book and reached for another.

Page after page that stated the legend of Cupid all had images of the same thing and with each one Cupid felt more and more enraged.

He was not a fucking cherub.

Watching the mortal was forgotten as Cupid ripped his way through multiple books.

It was safe to say Cupid was not a happy little bunny.

†

Belinda watched the last guy that had bugged her from her work leave, his head bowed. He seemed upset, why, she had no idea. All she had said was that she wasn't interested in his number and if he wasn't in the library for any other reason than looking up a book then it would be best if he left.

She couldn't help being a snarky cow, she had seriously had enough of the random men that would walk in and assume she would be interested. She wasn't so desperate that she would just take any guy up on his offer. It was so strange how, all of a sudden, men were going out of their way to talk to her or accost her.

At first she had been flattered; she had been over the moon that her wish had finally come true. Belinda had hoped that soon she wouldn't be labelled as the 'Virgin of the street' and maybe the trio would leave her alone and remove that profile from EHarmony.

She sighed, not that anyone had responded to that, but she had yet to look at said profile. Belinda didn't dare, she dreaded what they had written about her. Knowing those women it would say something like *Librarian beauty needs man in her life, 28 and not getting any younger. Respond quickly before she starts to sag.*

Belinda snorted and grinned, those women would do anything to help out, even if it did make her look a little stupid and desperate. She wasn't desperate she was just lonely; she wanted to snuggle up with someone at night. As long as they complied with her routine, that was, and didn't mess up her house. She shook her head and sighed, Belinda needed someone that would tolerate her issues and not get annoyed when she freaked out at what most people would call stupid stuff.

And that right there brought her focus back to Mike and the balls up she had performed the night before. What woman seriously brings up a random thing just after the guy she has fancied for ages finally locks lips with her? Oh yeah, that would be her.

Belinda shook her head then placed it on her arms on the desk. Today had just been brutal and she didn't think she could take much more. If one more bloke walked in and started asking random questions about love and romance books, all the while hinting for her number, she would snap.

A slam had her lifting her head, it sounded like a book had fallen but she couldn't see anything from where she was sat. She shrugged and then placed her head back onto her arms.

Mike… shit, she thought back to the night before again. After she had blurted out some crap about looking at the letter for her, he had made an excuse about needing to get home and had left quickly. So not only was she gifted at organisation, but she now could add running a guy out of her house in less than 10 minutes to her list of gifts and accomplishments.

His lips had felt amazing against her own and when he had laid her down she had finally managed to forget her anxiety about someone being in her house, or about tidying up. She had lost all train of thought and she had loved every second. She could recall, in perfect detail if she closed her eyes, the satisfaction on his face when he had pulled back to smile at her. His own eyes had blazed with need and that look had caused her butterflies to erupt into a flock of birds readying for take-off. She loved the fact his voice had dropped in tone and in that single moment, he hadn't stuttered. That alone meant he was just as lost as she was. That was until she had ballsed it up and opened her trap.

"Fucking idiot Belinda, that's what you are...An idiot."

Lifting her head, she picked up the letter, along with the small diary in the hopes she could make sense of both. The letter Mike had looked over, the night before, he had done more than google had but she still had the diary to read and after her putting her foot in it she didn't want to ask him to help her again. To be honest, even with the translation the contents of the letter were slightly confusing. *'Do not think lightly of this magical item'.* What the hell was she supposed to do with that?

Please be warned
Cupid's Essence is not what you think.
I warn you now, do not think lightly of this magical item. I happened upon it by chance.
Cupid created this, please believe me. It was made with the sole purpose to help find love.
It has done that, I agree, but it does so much more. But please be on your guard.
Choose wisely, for it has a mind of its own and it is not afraid to meddle, and it surely will.
Use it lightly I beg, the god means well but...
I must go...I pray love finds you.
Be well
Lady Marcella Rousseau

What the hell was she supposed to do with that? Cupid's Essence was just a perfume. How could it be anything else? But, then again, some things had happened since she had taken possession of the Essence that even she couldn't explain.

Belinda pulled the small diary towards her and opened it up to the first page. Because the diary was so small the entries were short, but still unreadable to her, until she attempted to translate it.

Dear Diary

Today I came upon a new perfume, it had been named Cupid's Essence and smelled of rainy summer nights. I purchased it on the spot; I could not resist the scent.

It called to me and I was helpless.

Strange though, the gentleman that sold it to me told me to be careful what I wish for. Why should I be careful? I just wish for what any girl wants.

A dashing man

Well, that and rich.

Marcella.

"Excuse me." A deep voice pulled Belinda's attention from the computer screen to that of a man stood at the desk. He looked hopeful and slightly cute. She just looked and then raised an eyebrow. She didn't talk, but instead waited for what was to come. Would he ask for books on romance or was he the brave type that would ask if the Karma Sutra was stocked?

Belinda watched as he calmly took some deep breaths and swallowed. He surprised her by asking directly for her number and not eating around the proverbial bush and asking for books he had no interest in.

"So, can I have your number?" He started out so well and Belinda actually considered handing her number over, until he let his mouth lose and ruined the moment.

"I've always wanted to date a librarian; it's always the quiet ones, eh?" he said, and grinned as he leaned on the counter and looked her up and down.

"I'm sorry?"

"Oh come on sweetie, you don't need to play sweet and innocent with me, we both know what's really beneath that innocent act."

Belinda bristled, then pushed her chair back to stand up. "Are you here for a book, sir?" she asked calmly, determined to remain professional. His attitude would have grated on her nerves anyway, but his arrogant assumption just pushed her full over the edge and into the shittiest mood ever. She folded her own arms and waited for an answer.

"Well?" she pushed when he didn't answer her

straight away, only to realise she had stretched her blouse by folding her arms and she was currently giving him a special glimpse at her cleavage. Immediately she let her arms drop and placed her hands on her hips. She wasn't going to bring attention to his ogling, she would ignore it completely.

"Err yeah, I'm here for a book and the names Clint by the way." He grinned and she dreaded his next words. "I'm here to check out the book of love."

He really said it. She wanted to bang her head on the desk but instead, she raised her hand and pointed towards the door.

"GET OUT!" she said, with enough force it echoed. She had said she couldn't take any more and this had been the last straw.

"What? You can't do that," he argued. "I'm here to get a book, you have to help me," he continued on.

Belinda walked around the desk until she was stood in front of him. Through clenched teeth she pressed out, "If you do not leave now, I will have you removed by force."

She became more irate as he folded his arms and leaned back against the counter. Shit, Belinda thought, how the fuck would she get him to leave now?

"You can't make me leave unless you give me your

number and agree to a date with me." He grinned again, assuming he had won. "Besides, you won't make me leave."

Belinda was about to argue, she wasn't sure how, but before she could take the breath in, another voice cut in and both had her excited and completely flummoxed at the same time.

"She won't make you leave, but I will." It was a voice she recognised, only, it was missing the stutter.

Belinda turned slightly to see Mike, looking like he had walked off the page of a Playgirl calendar, walk towards them. Dressed in his overalls, the top half had been tied around his waist and all he had covering his upper body was a black vest. The material clung to his chest muscles and with his arms free, she was able to see the bulging biceps. With each movement they flexed and caused an answering clench in her stomach. Belinda just stared.

"Mike."

Chapter Sixteen

Mike had spent the entire day watching men walk in and out of the library. It shouldn't have bothered him like it did, but each time he saw a bloke walk up to the doors he felt another knot in his shoulders tighten. He'd tried to roll them and loosen the muscles but it didn't help, he doubted even his physio could shift them. The only person that could help and loosen those knots was housed in that damn library and had been playing his feelings like a bloody harp.

He had finally plucked up the courage to go round to her house. He had made the move and had, for a brief moment in time, had her in his arms and responding to his kisses. When he had pressed her back on that sofa, all thought, except drowning himself in her taste, had eluded him. She had felt utterly perfect and fitted him like they had come from the same mould.

Yes, he had been turned on. Shit, what guy wouldn't be with her curvy body pressed up against his, her breasts pushing against his chest, and he could have sworn he had felt her nipples hard and erect. That thought alone had him thinking what she had been wearing under that blouse; there had definitely been no padding present.

Most of the day he had been glued to watching the window and had counted each man that had gone in, and then out. A part of him had been over the moon that each one had left looking dejected and forlorn. They could have been simply going in for a book, like most people would. But why would only guys go in? He had yet to see one woman walk in.

After the night before, he now felt a touch more possessive- or maybe just jealous- over Belinda. He knew after the abrupt ending to the evening that she would probably not want to see him again. But he could hope that she had been just as nervous as he was and had reacted in a way that wasn't positive to the situation. A situation that he hoped he would get another go at.

So here he was, stood in his overalls in the middle of the library staring down Clint, who he knew from the pub and who didn't seem to get the hint that he should leave. His gut instinct had told him to walk over to the library to talk to Belinda, and it was lucky he had. There was a fine line when it came to being forceful, especially with a woman, and he didn't doubt that Clint would cross it. For all Mike knew, Belinda could most likely look after herself, but Mike had been brought up to protect the fairer sex and he damn well would, especially one he more than just liked.

Clint just stood and stared at him. Mike knew he looked intimidating, he just hoped his little stutter issue would sod off whilst he sorted this. There was nothing like having his big hard man reputation ruined because he couldn't hold a sentence together in front of Belinda. He felt almost like Raj from *The Big Bang Theory*, unable to talk to women unless he was drunk, or in his case, horizontal on a sofa touching tongues.

But he had taken a chance, he had stupidly purchased a tonic from a gypsy after the rugby game last weekend, after she had told him that it would cure his pain in the ass stutter, now was the test to see if it truly did work, or if he had been ripped off by £50.

"Baby? You alright? You nearly ready to go?" he asked, and flicked his eyes to Belinda and felt a surge of triumph burst through him. She looked relieved and her answering smile, if anything else, would be payment enough.

"Yes, I'm just finishing up." She smiled more. "Let me just turn my computer off and fetch my bag," she blurted out, then turned to head towards her desk. Mike felt confident that Clint would take the hint and leave, instead, he reached out and grabbed Belinda's arm.

"Now wait just one second sweetheart, you haven't introduced us."

Mike wanted to growl at the sight of his hands on Belinda and he stepped forward. His voice was deep and husky as he said. "You want to remove your hand from my girl?"

His hands were now by his side and flexed as he felt anger start to simmer in his stomach. There had been only one other time in his life when he had let anger get the best of him. Since then he had kept a tight lid on it, but now… now he wanted to release it.

Mike kept his gaze locked on Clint as he repeated his request.

"I suggest you remove your hand." His voice was low and hard. Mike didn't dare take his gaze from Clint to look at Belinda. He didn't want to see her face, see the fear that this bell-end had caused or else his tight restrain would be broken.

The grip that Clint had on Belinda's arm, he could tell, was hurting her and he didn't doubt that it would leave a dark bruise, and that right there sent his pissed off level to the max. Clint's hand tightened ever so slightly and in turn, caused Belinda to let out a slight whimper of pain. As soon as she had made the sound he released her and held up his hands.

"Hey, no need to get angry mate."

"You are not my mate," Mike grated out as he watched Clint wink at Belinda who was rubbing her arm.

Clint then leaned back against the high desk.

Mike turned his focus back to Belinda, her eyes were wide with fear and she had now wrapped both arms around her waist, but otherwise she didn't move.

"Baby," he called out, and waited for her to turn her big blue-brown eyes his way. He smiled slightly as she finally turned towards him. "You want to go wait for me by the car, baby? I won't be long."

Mike waited, not sure if she would move at all until finally she turned and picked up her handbag from the counter, along with a large key. She made a great show of ignoring Clint as she walked past, head held high, only stopping slightly by Mike's side and placing a key within his palm.

With a lingering look, she walked out of the

library quickly, almost a run, but still dignified. Mike watched until she had left the building and the door had closed behind her before he turned his focus back to his new friend.

Chapter Seventeen

Mike had seen Clint quite a few times, he had been the guy who sat in the corner and watched the world go by with his solo pint of bitter. Here and now he looked completely different, but Mike couldn't quite put his finger on why. From what Gary had said, he was an insurance broker at one of the companies in town, and from his description, he would never say boo to a puppy, never mind have the balls to confront and grab a woman, or stand up to a guy Mike's size.

Something had changed, drastically. It was almost as if he had gained an inner confidence or had been somewhat possessed. If you looked into his eyes, you could see a quick intelligence that sent the hairs on the back of his neck to stand straight up.

Something was wrong and Mike didn't like the atmosphere at all, it was charged with testosterone and he felt like he was in a face-off with a guy that previously had shown no interest in Belinda before. Hell, everyone at the pub thought he was gay. This change in character was something that felt out of place and completely strange.

Not only that, but Mike was dealing with a sudden change to his own actions and that set him a little on edge. He had an overwhelming need and drive to protect Belinda, but also along with that, was an intense jealousy that was so foreign to Mike he was having a hard time controlling it. It was like all of his emotions, the good and the bad were intensified tenfold and there was little he could do to stop it.

Finally Clint moved away from the desk and approached Mike, who still had his hands fisted at his side concerned that the moment Clint came within reach he would have him by the throat. The smirk he had on his face was pushing Mike closer to the edge.

"Wow, the calm and collected Mike is all flustered over a bit of arse, which will definitely be something to share at the pub."

Clint patted Mike on the shoulder as he walked past. It took every bit of control Mike had to stop himself from laying him out flat on the floor. He kept himself still, determined to not let the twat rile him up.

"Don't worry, she's yours…Well, for now," Clint called out as he headed for the exit.

Mike kept his gaze locked straight forward until

the echo of Clint's footsteps had faded into silence. With deep calm breaths, Mike closed his eyes and waited, waited for the need to hurt and maim to pass and he felt more himself. He turned to leave, remembering to lock up with the key Belinda had given him. Maybe she had left straight away and headed home, but he hoped she had decided to wait.

He was both surprised and pleased to find Belinda not waiting by her car, but hidden on the driver's side to his truck. She was leant against the door, her head bowed and she was twisting a piece of tissue into shreds. Mike couldn't miss the intense shaking that seemed to overtake her body that accompanied intense sobs.

In a few strides, Mike stood in front of Belinda. With a gentle hand, he tipped her chin so he could see her face. In spite of the tears that had smudged her mascara and the red blotches on her face from the tears, she still looked stunningly beautiful. Mike couldn't speak; the need to take away anything that would cause her this amount of fear was intense. He wanted to be the one to protect her, and be the one she turned to when she felt afraid.

Without any thought to the possible repercussions, Mike bent his head and pressed his lips to hers. He tensed, fully expecting to be pushed away or slapped, and he wouldn't blame her if she did. But to his surprise her answer was to grab hold of his shirt and pull him closer, kissing him back with a passion he had never expected, well, not after their sofa session anyway.

He let her lead the way, letting her control this in a way she didn't have control of the earlier events, in a hope it would make her feel safe and make it known she would never have to fear him. With reluctance, Mike pulled away and was rewarded by a moan of denial. Resting his forehead against her own, neither of them moved or spoke until Mike reached around Belinda and grabbed the door handle to the truck.

"Come on, let's get you home," he said quietly and waited for her to nod in agreement. They both stepped back from the truck and Mike opened the door, letting Belinda in the driver's side and watched her climb over the gear stick to the passenger seat. Yes, they could have used the other door, but neither one of them were currently thinking straight. Mike quickly slid behind the wheel and started the engine before he easily manoeuvred the truck out of the car park and onto the main road.

✝

Clint watched with jealous eyes as Mike had kissed Belinda before he had bundled her into his truck and had driven off. A rage Clint had never before felt, nor thought he was capable of, had taken root inside and now wanted to explode outwards. He no longer felt in control of his body, nor his feelings. In fact, he felt like a bystander, someone on the sidelines, watching, but with zero control and as much as he enjoyed the anger that simmered within him, he also felt fear. This wasn't him; his actions had just proved that.

Clint had never been one to approach a woman like Belinda, never mind grab hold of her and become borderline abusive. His mother had made it a point to bring him up with a healthy respect of how to treat people.

After he had watched the black truck disappear up the road, Clint made his way to his own car. Sliding into the driver's seat of the Volvo, he pulled down the sun visor to look into the mirror. Instead of his usual muddy green orbs, bright blue reflected back at him and a hard, deep voice filled his head.

His body stopped responding to his commands and Clint felt his own consciousness being pushed to the back of his mind as a new presence took over.

"Don't worry Clint, I will take it from here."

The voice scared Clint as his own face smiled back in the reflection; his appearance changed and looked menacing. The Volvo started and the engine revved before the car pulled out of the car park as Clint's presence shrank away, leaving only the newcomer in control.

With no control, he could only watch as idea after idea formed inside his head, ones that frightened him with their darkness. Only a part of him revelled in them, opened up the part of him that enjoyed the darker side of life and called to that small, dark stain on his soul. The presence, along with himself, wanted Belinda. Clint forgot his previous fear and embraced his new fate, ready and eager to be of use.

Chapter Eighteen

The drive back to her house was quiet and Belinda didn't try to push any conversation, she had only just managed to stop the shaking that had overtaken her body as soon as she had left the library. Her hands were now the only extremity that continued to shake. Belinda had fisted them into her blouse in an attempt to stop it, but it was like they had a mind of their own. She bit her lip and tried to stop her mind from racing. The events of the afternoon span around in her mind, what ifs circled in her skull.

Like, what if Mike hadn't have shown up when he did, would she have been able to fend off Clint's advances on her own? What if Clint had become more angry? What if… What if!!!

Belinda would admit that she knew nothing of self-defence, which was exceptionally foolish on her part. She should have known a situation like what had happened could have happened, but no, she foolishly believed that she would never have to deal with anything like that.

A small movement to her right had Belinda flinching, only to relax as Mike reached over and tugged her right hand free from the material of her blouse then interlocked their fingers together. He kept his eyes glued to the road the entire time and changed gears using his own right hand, all so he could maintain constant contact with Belinda. This small gesture meant the world to her and it cemented his place in her heart.

Mike rubbed his thumb over the skin of her hand, his own engulfed hers but not once did she ever feel threatened by his size. He always made her feel protected. Belinda looked at their joint fingers then up to Mike's face. She had never truly taken the time to study Mike. Although she did fancy him they had never been in such close proximity before. From the side, Belinda could make out how slightly crooked his nose was and that his left ear seemed swollen. His hair curled in that annoying way that made every woman jealous as they could never replicate it.

Mike's lower lip looked bigger and a little bit out of proportion to the rest of his face. To Belinda, though, all of these small things weren't flaws but made him even more appealing to her. She watched as his gaze flicked to hers then back to the road, and a small smirk tweaked at his lips. Bloody hell, the man had dimples as well, Belinda thought, as her stomach did a flip. He was a great big hunk of sexy and she could spend hours just mapping his features.

The silence continued even as Mike pulled his hand free from hers to pull the truck to a stop right outside her house. He cut the engine but didn't say a word, they both sat there in the light of the street lamp. Being only 4:30pm it was surprisingly dark but the street itself was quiet with little or no traffic.

"Thank you," Belinda whispered.

He didn't respond, so she turned a little in her seat and faced him.

"Thank you Mike, I dread to think what would have happened had you not turned up." As soon as Belinda had said the words out loud her body started to shake again.

With no word, Mike unhooked his seat belt and slid his seat right back before he unhooked her belt. Belinda gasped loud as Mike reached over and grabbed her by the waist. As gently as possible, he pulled her over the gear stick and onto his lap, her knees straddled his waist and pushed her skirt up so it barely covered her arse. Belinda's hands immediately flew to grab hold of his broad shoulders for balance, but another gasp was pulled from her as her core settled against his own groin, her plain panties and his jeans all that separated her from a very hard and large cock.

Her previous shakes forgotten, Belinda looked down into Mike's face and into his eyes. This time she could see all of his features from the front, she could make out every lump and bump on his nose and cheek, ones from the battering he took playing rugby. His lips that, from the side looked out of proportion, looked perfect to her and his eyes drew her in.

"Belinda," Mike breathed, and she was lost. "No need to thank me, baby." His voice low and husky, it seemed to caress every nerve in her body.

"But if you hadn't-"

"Shhhhhh," he stopped her mid-sentence. "Don't over think it."

Belinda nodded but didn't say anything else. He was right, though, she always tended to over think or over analyse things and it always made them out to be worse than what they really were. It was how her OCD operated, except for when she was with Mike. In the few times they had been alone together, she noticed she seemed more settled and that surprised Belinda most of all. She had struggled her whole life to fit in and this man helped her feel almost normal just by sitting near her.

"Can I kiss you again, Belinda?" Mike's voice broke through the fog of her thoughts. It was even lower than before and completely devoid of his stutter. Belinda knew if she opened her mouth now something stupid and completely random would fly out and ruin the moment, so she took her father's advice; she kept her mouth shut this one time and, as before, she nodded in response. If she didn't control herself somehow and learn to act like a sane person she would be doomed to spend the rest of her days doing the Churchill dog impression. Her chin never even made an inch before Mike smiled.

Shit a brick, Belinda thought, that smile changed everything. Forgotten were any imperfections he might have, because the man had dimples. She was transfixed as his handsome face became downright gorgeous. Was her mouth hanging open? Belinda really didn't care if it was. Hell, you would have to be dead to not respond to that, and this man wanted to kiss her. That thought right there sobered Belinda up and made her heart start beating fast, like she was running.

Belinda never moved as Mike slid his left hand around her waist and tugged her closer, whilst the other slid behind her head and pulled her closer to his lips.

"Mike, wait, everyone can see us through the windows." She pressed against his chest slightly, only to hear him chuckle and she became transfixed, once again, at the way his lips moved as he talked. A hint of white teeth peeked out with each word and his breath hinted at mint and coffee.

"Tinted windows Belinda, no one can see a thing." His lips were a mere few inches from her own and she could hear her own heartbeat in her ears. Would he taste as good as he did the other night? Would it be as intense? All these thoughts rattled around in her head.

"Stop thinking so hard," he whispered, a moment before his lips touched her own and Belinda closed her eyes to savour the pleasure that was to come.

With Belinda's eyes shut, she relied on her other senses and fell into the kiss. Her hands kneaded his shoulders in a similar way a cat did. A groan flew from her mouth, surprising her. The sound seemed to excite Mike as he pulled her even closer to him, crushing her breasts against his chest.

The heated ambience in the cab of the truck had thickened; steam from their combined body heat had already fogged up the windows. The temperature was steadily rising and in comparison to the icy weather outside, Belinda felt cocooned in heat and passion.

Evidence that Mike was enjoying their kiss as much as her pressed hard and hot against her almost exposed core. Instead of scaring someone of her innocence, it excited her. Belinda felt empowered. What woman of 28 wouldn't when she was currently straddling a beast of a man with her tongue down his throat and her foo about as close to his gentlemen's area as it could get without, well, you know.

This had been the closest Belinda had ever been to a guy and she now knew- well, she had a hint now, at what she had missed. The feelings Mike evoked within her made her feel sexy and wanted. Belinda may be a virgin but that didn't equate to being stupid, and like every other woman on the planet, she got horny. But in this moment she felt on fire, her moans, uninhibited, erupted from her mouth as she moved her hands to cup Mike's face and attempted to take control over the kiss.

Her hips moved over his huge, hard length and he bucked in response, hitting her in the perfect place that almost had her eyes rolling to the back of her head in pleasure. Belinda couldn't help but mewl in disappointment as Mike pulled away from the kiss.

"Fuck baby," he croaked out, almost unable to get

his words out. His voice was a low growl and the look in his eyes had Belinda's stomach flipping. It was a look of utter possession, and it excited her.

"You feel so damn good," he whispered into her ear, just before he licked the skin behind it and then took the lobe between his teeth and tugged. With no stutter to distract her from the richness of his voice, each word flowed over her and caused every hair on her body to stand on end.

The stutter had always made him seem sort of vulnerable but now he was the complete opposite. Mike was all huge, hard body and dominant attitude. Before Mike, she would have avoided those traits like the plague but now he ticked every box, even the ones she didn't know she had.

"I want you Belinda, I always have," he began, his voice and breath caressing her ear and causing her to shiver. Belinda closed her eyes as his heated words elicited a fantasy in her mind.

"I want to strip you baby. Oh so slowly, take every single piece of clothing from your body until I can see every perfect inch of your creamy skin laid out before me."

Belinda's chest heaved and her hands once again moved, they made the journey back from his face down to his shoulders and she gripped them hard.

"Fuck Belinda, I want you. I want to taste you so bad my mouth waters at the thought," he purred into her ear.

She couldn't contain the gasp as his large, calloused hand slid up her bare thigh. Belinda hadn't been aware it had moved at all, but now she shook in excitement. The touch of his bare skin on hers caused an electric-type shock that travelled from her leg to her core. She felt his fingertips graze her panty covered core and fought for breath.

"I want to see how wet you are for me baby."

Belinda shook with pleasure as his words ignited image upon image in her head; fantasies of them together blended and melded, making it hard for her to breathe. His touch almost burned, but she loved each and every slide of skin on skin. Her hips bucked in an attempt to keep constant contact.

She felt lost in the sea of passion and pleasure and would surely drown if it wasn't for the beacon of light at the back of her mind that fought to ignore Mike's drugging kisses and licks and his mind blowing touches to her most private of areas. That spark, although tiny, reminded her she was still a virgin and as such, maybe the best place for her first time wasn't the front seat of Mike's truck.

She fought against the part of her that didn't want

to stop; she wanted the high feeling of pleasure to go on and on.

"Mike," she panted. "Mike, please stop a second." Her voice sounded foreign to her, she had never before sounded husky and a tad sexy.

She felt Mike stiffen and slowly pull his mouth away from her neck, his hand moved from between her legs to rest on her thigh and his eyes met hers as he waited for her to continue. His face held a hint of regret and remorse, which was unexpected. She had expected to see anger at having been made to stop, but the regret pulled at her and made her realise that if she didn't say something soon she would ruin this moment and any future moments.

"I'm sorry, I shouldn't have behaved that way," Mike said in a low voice, regret laced each word and tugged on Belinda's heart.

Belinda also knew that if she said the wrong thing, everything she hoped for between the two of them could be ruined. The atmosphere was already changing, she never wanted what was happening between them to end, but she also wanted to be completely honest with Mike, especially about her current sexual status.

"Mike wait, please." She placed both her hands on his cheeks, making sure their eyes met and she had his full attention. "Please don't be sorry." She smiled and kissed his lips once more, feeling strangely confident. "Your touch does things to me."

Belinda blushed but didn't let her embarrassment stop her; she ploughed on, "I enjoy your touch so much. I didn't want it to stop."

She could see that Mike was about to ask why she had indeed stopped then, so she blurted it out before he had a chance to question her. Divulging a secret not many people were aware of.

"I'm a virgin, Mike."

She waited in silence, their breathing the only noise to fill the truck. She had never, ever pictured giving that information this way, but it was out in the open now. Belinda watched Mike's face as he processed it all, his face actually not changing; only his eyes flickered from a sadness to something else she had only ever seen once.

The look in his eyes matched the one Clint had in his earlier that day, but with Mike it felt different and she enjoyed it. But, then again, she had never, ever pictured herself straddled across Mike's lap in the front seat of his truck going at it like teenagers did. Her day had been full of firsts; she just hoped she hadn't hindered a second and a third.

Chapter Nineteen

Mike was stunned. Had he heard her right? He continued to look over her face, searching for anything that would give any indication that she was bullshitting him. But as he looked deeper into her bright eyes, he saw nothing but honesty. Her bright red cheeks, even noticeable in the dull lights of the street lamps, showed she felt more embarrassed than anything else.

"A virgin," he repeated.

Belinda nodded and then whispered, "Yes".

Mike's hands tightened their grip on her thigh and waist, his fingers dug in slightly. He didn't want to break any connection with her. In fact, he wanted her closer than she was currently; a feat that was impossible.

The information wasn't much to process, but its meaning meant more to him than Belinda would ever know. It was a sign of trust. Hell, her being on his lap in his truck showed that she must somehow trust him. But for her to open up, stop him and tell him straight, just made him respect the hell out of her. What she had just divulged wasn't general knowledge or else it would have been well known at the pub.

Men actually gossiped more than women did and anything like that would go through the town like flu. Nearly every single- and some married- guys in town all at some point had the hots for his Belinda. It drove him mad when they made comments about her, and he had been thankful that none had made an attempt to ask her out. Most didn't have the balls. Belinda had been nicknamed the "ice queen" since she had shown zero emotion to any guy that had tried. Well, she wasn't ice that was for sure. He had been lucky in the sense she had turned to him to help her with his car and not one of his work mates. He liked to think it was because she liked him too.

"Mike?" she asked quietly, and he realised he had been silent for far too long. She would be, no doubt, thinking that he would be put off when, in fact, it was the complete opposite.

"Belinda, baby it's ok."

"Really?" she answered. "You aren't laughing at me or put off?"

"Fuck no," he exclaimed, and moved his hands to take hers from his face, kissing her palms. "Gods, woman!" He grinned and kissed her fingers. "Do you not realise how fucking happy that makes me?"

"What! Really?" she said once again, confused by his response.

Mike nodded back as he stroked her small hands, running his fingers across the soft skin.

"Yes baby, just knowing you want to give even a small piece of yourself to me brings out a side of me I thought had been locked away."

"You like the fact that I'm a virgin…" Belinda answered, still confused by his reaction.

Mike chuckled and pulled her arms around his neck before he moved his own arms around her waist and tugged her closer once more. He kissed the tip of her nose before he explained what it was that didn't repulse or make him not want to be there with her.

"I like it a lot, honey. I like the fact no other man has touched you." Mike pressed a kiss to her lips. "No other man had been inside of you or has made you scream out in pleasure."

Once again he kissed her lips and enjoyed her simple answer of "uh huh" and felt her shake. He loved that she was so affected by his words.

"Does that make me a caveman Belinda? That I want to be the only one to do those things to you, over and over again." He could feel her breaths on his face as they increased in pace.

"Belinda," he breathed, and moved his lips to travel down her neck once again. He would show her how good it was between them and that she could trust him. "Let me show you how good I can make you feel." He bit down on her earlobe, loving her gasp and quiet groan. "Say yes baby."

Her whispered "yes" fired Mike's heart rate up and pulled a groan from his own lips. Sliding his hands to palm her buttocks, he pulled her forward and tight against his hard length that strained against his jeans. Her hips bucked and forced Mike to suck in a breath. The heat her pussy gave off against his cock was intense and he fought the need to rip his zip open and free himself. It took all he had to stop, but this time was for Belinda. He would gain her trust, no matter how much time it took, and that alone gave him the control he needed.

Mike wrapped his left arm around her waist, keeping her pressed against him, and slid his right hand back down her body and up her bare thigh. Her skin was like silk to the touch and quivered as his fingers quickly found the seam of her panties.

He moved his fingers up and down over the material, feeling how soaked she had already become. He had done this, he had made her wet with desire, and she wanted him. He growled into her ear as he moved the material to the side and swept his finger across her pussy, collecting the juices.

"Fuck, you are soaked baby." His fingers moved up to her engorged clit and flicked the nub. Her hips once again bucked. "So fucking wet and all mine." He growled again and moved his fingers against her clit in a circular motion, massaging the nub and pulling groans of pleasure from Belinda's lips. Her nails dug into his shoulders and he grinned, knowing she was becoming lost in the pleasure he was giving her.

"You want more, baby?" Mike asked, and stopped his massage, instead placing pressure on her clit. He wanted her to say out loud she wanted more. He wanted her moans louder in his ears. Damn, he wanted *everything* she had to give. Every scream and gasp of pleasure belonged to him. He had the rights and he would damn well collect the royalties.

"Tell me you want more, Belinda." He felt her nod a few times as if she couldn't quite get the words out and her hips moved, eager for him to continue his ministrations, so Mike stopped the pressure and pulled her once again tighter to him. If she kept up moving like this on his lap, he would explode before he even had her half way to an orgasm. He was a man after all and he had pride, so blowing his load before her was not an option.

"Say the words baby, I want to hear you say it," he growled out and pulled his head back to look at her face. Another grin spread across his own as he looked at the dazed expression on Belinda's face. Her eyes were at half-mast and her lip was swollen from being chomped on by her teeth. Her hair was down now, messy and framing her beautiful face. It made his heart ache. But he wanted his words.

"Belinda." He waited for her to open her eyes, he was desperate to continue but she had to ask.

"Say it, baby." She finally opened her eyes and started to chew on her lip once again. Her cheeks were red from the heat they had created and, he guessed, from a little hint of shyness at being asked to say the words. He pushed once more.

"Baby…" Her voice, when she answered, was breathy and had a husky tone to it.

"More," she whispered. "Mike, please I ache."

Mike growled and melded his lips to hers as soon as the words had left her mouth. His fingers continued to assault her clit as he moved more of his palm underneath the material.

"Baby," he whispered against her lips. "You trust me to make you feel good, yeah?"

Belinda nodded as he felt her hands sink into his hair and scrape her nails across his scalp.

"Good," he grinned. "Hold on baby."

Gently at first, Mike caressed and massaged her clit until he found the exact spot that made her groan and shake the most. He would have loved to sink his fingers deep inside her pussy and make her scream, but he didn't want to push her too much, too fast.

Mike's own pleasure increased as she became more and more vocal in her pleasure and her hips started to buck in time to the movement of his fingers. Belinda felt amazing in his arms and the images of when he would finally get to sink deep inside her in this position nearly sent him over the edge.

Focusing on Belinda, he increased his pace once more; along with sliding her across the bulge of his hard cock. He knew she was close and there was nothing he wanted more than to hear and see her erupt. He pulled his lips away and watched as her head fell backwards and she moaned, her mouth open as she fought for breaths.

"You close, baby?" Mike asked, and was rewarded by a nod and another moan from Belinda. She was so close, her whole body was shaking and her hips bucked even quicker. Mike moved his thumb and forefinger taking her clit and pinching hard at the same time he whispered into her ear.

"Come for me baby, let me hear you." He pinched again and then pressed, pinched and pressed until her body stiffened.

Mike watched as her head fell back, her eyes closed and a deep, husky moan erupted from her mouth as she fell over the edge, into her climax. It was the most beautiful thing Mike had ever seen. She was a goddess in his eyes and his heart ached that it had taken him this long to get her in his arms.

This would be where she stayed.

Her hips kept moving and Mike could do nothing but ride the wave of pleasure as it hit him. With her neck exposed, he leaned forward, pressed a kiss to the skin where her shoulder joined her neck then bit down, hard. Not enough to break the skin but enough that she gasped then moaned again. Mike growled into her skin as his own climax hit. Emptying himself into his jeans, he struggled to catch his breath.

Gently, Mike removed his hand from her panties and once again wrapped both arms around her waist and pulled her close. Their foreheads met and so did their eyes, no embarrassment could be seen on Belinda's face as she smiled shyly at him. This was what

Mike had been missing in his life, a passionate, beautiful woman who made his heart ache and his head pound. He kissed her lips gently, mindful they were swollen.

"Fuck," he growled out and was answered by Belinda's giggled response.

"You can say that again."

Chapter Twenty

Cupid sat, once more perched on a surface. This time on the brick wall of a large town house just down the road from where his chosen mortal was having her jollies rocked. It was about time if you asked him. But who was he to comment on modern mortals wanting to stay untouched? Really, he should find out her name, but then again, that made the whole ordeal a little bit more personal and he was already in a bit deeper than he should be. Never mind *him* putting Psyche on a sex ban, the way shit was going, if she found out *he* would be banned, or worse.

Shaking his head, Cupid tried to focus on the task at hand but the mere thought of Psyche banning him access to her lagoon of splendour or even trying to hurt *Pedro* was at the back of his mind. A man's Mandangle was his pride and joy; they were soulmates, never apart.

"It's ok Pedro, I won't let anything happen to

you," he crooned at his crotch. No one got between Cupid and his *Pedro*.

He looked once again down the road to the black truck that now sported steamed up windows and, to his sensitive hearing, moans of pleasure could be heard. Maybe now she would see what she was missing. It wouldn't surprise him in the slightest if she started demanding an orgasm a day. Not that he would blame her. As the epitome of love he would encourage it and believed every man and woman should, in short, get their rocks off daily. He did.

Cupid grinned. He had earlier and his beautiful wife was now in receipt of a detailed video of the event. He had hopes she would react to it better than his special picture.

In a perfect world, she would be waiting for him stark bollock naked with only a pair of red killer heels on and bent over the kitchen counter after baking a tray of double chocolate chip muffins. No wait, not naked, he chuckled in his head. She would be wearing a pinny and the heels.

"Bloody hell Pedro, that is hot shit right there."

Cupid shook his head to shake free of the new fantasy and tried to focus on what he was supposed to be doing in the current moment. He was starting to understand now when Psyche said he had the attention span of a goldfish.

The couple were still in the truck and this made Cupid smile. *This* was what the mortal female needed, a man that would take control and treat her right.

The male would, that Cupid had seen. The man had given his heart to the female- that was obvious. All that was left was for Belinda to open her heart to him, only then would the Essence become devoid of power.

The problem was, until then, she would continue to garner the interest of other males. Maybe that would work in her favour, though. The male seemed to be very protective over her. Cupid could hope; he didn't have long before his wife would be checking up on him and if she found out he had interfered again… Well, he was not prepared for a spanking ban at all.

Swinging his legs, Cupid looked up at the sky, watching the stars. It was the little things in life that the mortals now missed and took for granted. How many actually sat down and took stock of the important things like love, and family and companionship?

Upon looking back at the truck, he couldn't help but laugh as he watched the female get out of the vehicle and try to smooth her clothes out. She turned and looked up at the huge male who had rocked her socks off. Another passionate kiss ensued and Cupid smiled. Right there was his reason: love and passion. No one should have that missing from their lives.

They exchanged more words; a promise of meeting in the pub later, and then she left and went into the building. The male watched her go in before he adjusted himself- which made Cupid snort- got back into his truck and drove down the road to his own property.

Cupid again used his god-like abilities to hide himself from mortal eyes. Or what he liked to call his very own 'Spidey senses', only he shot a completely different stream of white stuff than the famous Spiderman did, and if he ever decided to don an all in one lycra suit, he would look a dam sight sexier too.

Pedro didn't like Lycra though, so Cupid's dream of being a superhero was dashed in the conception. Cupid once again shook his head, yet again he had become distracted by random thoughts, but he was happy to see the spell would be soon drawing to a close so the prospect of getting caught was becoming slimmer. So he would go home and pretend he had been a good boy all this time.

"Cupid! It's been a while," a low voice called out from the shadows of the building he was sat in front of. It had Cupid jumping from the wall. Although he was still wearing his favourite grey joggers he was still a formidable figure and one most wouldn't fuck with.

"Show yourself," he demanded. There weren't many beings in the world that would be able to see him whilst he was cloaked; only fellow gods and a handful of mortals had that ability. He didn't like the fact he could be seen, as that may just ruin his chances of getting away with his scheme scot-free.

He watched as a young male stepped from the shadows and into the light of a street lamp. Cupid recognised him as the male that had got a little too handsy with his mortal in the library. This was no normal mortal male- that was obvious; his eyes held a god-like glow and his aura swirled with hints of black and gold. This mortal was possessed and Cupid had a bloody good idea who by.

"Apollo," he said calmly. "Didn't think I would see you around for a while. How's the underworld treating you?"

"Tut, tut, tut, you really shouldn't speak to your elders that way."

"How about you kiss my peachy, pert buttocks?" Cupid answered, and folded his beefy arms across his chest.

"No need to be testy," Apollo replied, and then

grinned. Cupid felt for the mortal that had become prey to this god's interference and hoped there was something he could do to help. But love was his forte, not battle; although he was always up for a good brawl.

Cupid was already well aware of Apollo's situation. Gossip was rife within Olympus and Psyche always gave him the run down when she got home from lunch with the ladies. Turns out Apollo had been a very bad boy and had pissed off a few gods and mortals, and had been banished to the fields of punishment. Apollo had gained power from somewhere to be able to possess a mortal body and that alone didn't bode well for the mortal, or Cupid's plan of staying off the radar.

"Is there something you want Apollo? I am rather busy; I have plans that include *The Great British Bake Off*, buttercream and baby oil."

"Enough!" Apollo called out and walked closer. "You should have more respect for the elder gods of Olympus, Cupid. Although, you can't really class yourself as a god, can you? You are more a shadow of Aphrodite really, not even worthy of the status of god," Apollo sneered out and walked back towards the shadows and away from Cupid.

Whatever the sun god's plan was, Cupid wasn't

really fazed. His words were those he had heard many a time and was one of the many reasons why he never ventured to Olympus, if he could help it. If Apollo thought to anger him, he would be mistaken, but if he made him miss tonight's episode of *Bake Off* then shit would most definitely go down.

"You quite finished?" Cupid asked. "If you were expecting me to blow smoke up your arse then you are sorely mistaken. I couldn't give a shit what you think. After all, I'm not the one trapped in the under-world and having to rely on the possession of a mortal to do my bidding, am I?"

Cupid unfolded his arms and stepped forward. He knew that he could often be selfish, but this god took it to a whole new level. Apollo had messed with his family, his fellow gods. And as much as they annoyed him with whatever shit they had going on in Olympus that would eventually filter down to him, Apollo's actions in trying to harm them pissed him off.

Cupid wasn't scared of Apollo, there was little he could do whilst trapped in the mortal.

in the mortal; he just worried what his plan would be, as he had also targeted his mortal.

"Why are you here, Apollo?" Cupid asked bluntly.

"My, my, someone has big balls, don't they?" Apollo taunted. "My reason for being here will become clear, Cupid. But, if you are going to go running to your creator then let her know she won't always win." He smirked, turned on his heel and walked down the street with a swagger that made Cupid twitch.

Apollo had a serious issue with Aphrodite and now he had involved Cupid. He wasn't sure if Apollo was stupid or just plain batshit crazy, because no one messed with love and got away with it.

If there was ever a time where Cupid needed to be on the ball and stop getting distracted, this was it, but it also meant he may have to admit to his little plan. With that in mind, Cupid made his way back to his home; he had some thinking and preparing to do. The safety of his mortal came first and he would be there to make sure his plan went off without an issue.

Chapter
Twenty-One

Belinda sat at her kitchen table and tried to stop the shaking of her hands, nervous was an understatement to how she was feeling at that very moment. Ever since she had left the truck, and Mike, she had been in a whirlwind of emotion.

What they had done in the truck should make her feel shy and embarrassed but, in fact, she felt alive and strangely different. So she had showered, but that had turned out to take longer than she had expected. Images of what Mike had done with his gifted fingers had assaulted her so she had ended up bringing herself to release in the shower, moaning into the tiles, actually wishing it was Mike touching her instead. Her climax had felt empty in comparison to what she had felt in the truck, and she now craved more. Her new discovery scared and excited her and the thought of finally getting rid of her virgin status no longer frightened her as it used to.

Her body felt more alive than it had ever done in

the past. Mike had awakened something and she was eager to test the limits of her new awareness. A part of Belinda wondered if the Essence had something to do with what was happening, but she wouldn't deny it even if it did. She was thankful, because it had finally pushed her to the one she had been drawn to, but had no idea how to go about getting his attention.

So here she sat, dressed up, more so than she had done in years and her stomach was rolling. Compared to what she had just got up to with Mike, a date shouldn't be scary at all. But she would have to talk to him and she had little doubt that she would say something stupid and make herself look like an idiot.

Her outfit she had picked out had been one she had bought, but never had the guts to wear. A long black pencil skirt that sat high on her waist with a sleeveless red V-necked blouse, this was finished off with blank ankle boots that had cost her a small fortune back when she had bought them. But the whole outfit somehow made her feel confident and a little sexy.

She had gone all out and left her hair down, even curling a few of the wayward strands as well as donning some make-up that highlighted her eyes and lips, but wasn't too full on. She didn't often wear make-up but she wanted to look as good as she could for tonight. She had a gut feeling that the evening would change everything, her stomach wouldn't settle and that was either nerves getting the better of her or she had suddenly gained the skills Lassie and Skippy had been famous for...

Belinda smiled as her bag started to vibrate again; it had been doing that off and on since she got home, as if it was happy and excited for her. That was the Essence, it seemed to have a consciousness all of its own and would react to the situation at hand. She liked it, it felt like she had a friend and she had found she spoke to it a lot, especially in the last few days.

Belinda tapped the table about five times before she pressed off it and stood. Her boots clicked across the tile as she picked up her small leather jacket from the counter, and her handbag, before she walked to the door.

"Come on girl, you can do this."

She looked at herself in the mirror next to the front door, not recognising herself at all. She hadn't since the day the Essence had come home. It was like it had tapped into something deep down, something she had never shown anyone else.

"Belinda, you can do this, just think of... shit, I don't know. But defo don't think of his dimples or the fact you fancy the crap out of him or you will fuck this up." She smiled and nodded at her reflection and without waiting, threw open the door and headed out into the street.

The pub was only a couple of hundred yards down the road from where they both lived which meant it would make things a little easier and they could both have a drink which suited her just fine. The term Dutch courage was flying through her head, but she reckoned shit faced drunk would be a step too far. A cheeky little shot once she got there wouldn't do any harm...she hoped. Belinda was more concerned with what random tripe her mouth would erupt with, either that or she would sit there like a mute and just smile and nod.

Ahh shit, Belinda thought. Could she do this? Yes, she could. She smiled as the Essence vibrated in agreement in her bag, almost egging her on.

"The Vicar's Pulpit." Belinda snorted at the name, whoever had named the place was clearly trying to be all serious but in this day and age, most would find the rude side

She laughed then mentally pulled up her big girl panties (and her thong) and pushed through the door, into the bar area of the pub.

Even though there was a smoking ban on public areas, this seemed to be the only pub she knew of that still let their patrons spark up inside. Belinda tried not to cough as she walked in but, instead, inhaled too much of someone's cigar and started her evening hacking up a lung.

"You alright there, Miss?" the bar man called. "Can I help you?"

"Yeah." She coughed and walked towards the bar, aware and slightly uneasy about the stares she was getting.

Belinda looked behind her then forward again, her nerves hitting a high that she didn't think even Mike's presence would solve.

"Can I have a gin and tonic, oh, and also a shot of tequila, please?" she asked nervously.

The barman was, at first, taken aback then nodded with a smile. "Sure thing, honey. You all alone?" he asked as he started on her drinks.

"Not for long," she replied. "I have a date," Belinda said with more courage than she felt.

"Lucky fella," he answered, with almost a sulk. She would have laughed and felt flattered at any other time but something felt off, the atmosphere in the pub didn't feel right and she had feeling she was being stared at a lot. But she was too nervous to turn around.

The hairs on the back of her neck started to

prickle as she felt someone approach the bar.

"Let me get this for the lady, Barry."

Belinda went to answer but was stopped as another gentleman appeared on her other side.

"No, I will pay for her drinks Barry, ignore the fool."

She didn't say anything but stood between two guys that, she would say, were slightly older than her. They argued back and forth until another slipped in next to her and winked whilst handing over a ten pound note to the barman.

"Too late, I got this."

"Oi!" one shouted and pushed the third man.

Belinda felt trapped and tried to make a move so she could go and sit on her own, but the room seemed all of a sudden too small and far too crowded. She felt hands push and pull at her as they went from arguing about who could buy her drinks to who could ask her out. Their voices became louder as more men joined in, wedging her against the bar.

In her bag the Essence vibrated hard, almost in warning, just as a fist was thrown and a full on brawl broke out.

Being jostled against the bar, Belinda winced and almost cried out. She would no doubt sport a large bruise once she got home, if she ever got home. With nowhere else to go, Belinda pushed back against the men behind her then jumped up onto the bar. She was now able to see over what she would describe as a hoard of men that were beating seven bells of shit out of each other, and she wasn't even sure why. Hands grabbed at her legs as some of them noticed she no longer stood near them.

"Hey, don't go," one shouted, and tried to grab her skirt, ripping it as he tugged, leaving Belinda with a large slit up one side.

"Let go of me," she shouted, only to find another attempt to grab her arm.

"We want to show you a good time," another said.

Reaching behind her, Belinda found the handle of the broom that had been left propped up against the side of the bar. She fought off the grabbing hands and knelt on the bar and with more gusto then she ever showed in Physical Education at school, she started to smack each man that approached her on the head with her new weapon.

"I only bloody came here for a date with Mike." SMACK, SMACK. "And you've all fucking ruined it!" SMACK, SMACK.

"And where is MIKE?" she screamed as she smacked another.

Chapter
Twenty-Two

The sight that greeted Psyche's eyes as she walked into the bar stunned the living crap out of her. What in the name of all that was holy had gone on? Luckily, she had managed to freeze events and now everyone was stood and looked like they were taking part in the mannequin challenge.

Seriously, she thought, she leaves for a small getaway with the girls and bam! Cupid starts acting like a complete moron again. How many times had she warned him what happened when he got personally involved? Now she stood, looking at the issues he had caused and she wasn't happy. It would take more than just Cupid's cocky bastard smile to get him his man card back this time.

She sighed and turned to survey the damage, damage meaning the destruction of the bar caused by one potent love spell on one small mortal female who, she didn't think, had asked for it.

She was beautiful, you couldn't miss that, but she

could tell the spell had worked its wonders on bringing her out of her shell and showing not only the world, but herself, the goddess she was inside. That was the issue with women in this day and age; there was a preconception that women had to look and act a certain way and for some, that pressure drove them to hide their true selves from everyone.

This mortal had blossomed but, as was the nature of Cupid's fuck ups, that blossom had been followed by a storm. Every single male that came within a hundred foot radius of the mortal would feel a tug, forcing them to alter their route or path and, in essence, meet with the intended. She had seen this spell done before, but not for a very long time.

"Cupid, you sneaky little bastard, come out now," Psyche called out. She stood in her favourite skinny jeans, thigh high boots and blue blouse with her hands on her hips. To say that she was annoyed wouldn't quite cover it. This was the last thing she wanted to deal with when she got home. She had thought, after all this time, Cupid would have learned.

"Love bug, you are home!"

Psyche slowly turned to the direction of the voice, not surprised to see he was half dressed in a pair of grey joggers. She raised an eyebrow and he tried to act all innocent.

"Miss me, baby?" he crooned, and instead of the kiss he no doubt wanted, she poked him in the nose with her finger.

"What the fuck have you done, Cupid? Have you not seen the cluster fuck that is this bar?"

"I don't know what you mean, twiddle thumbs."

"DO NOT act dumb with me." She poked his nose once more. "I know your handy work when I see it, Cupid, and not forgetting the shiny pink heart over that mortal which gives you away, so stop bull-shitting me."

Psyche folded her arms across her chest and waited for Cupid to answer. After a moment, she had to snap her fingers in his face.

"Cupid, I swear I will cause Pedro severe damage that may take millennia to heal from if you do not answer me." He nodded, but he eyes were fixated on her breasts as they were pushed against the fabric of her blouse.

"Come here Wife, let me slay your nipples with my tongue."

"Oi, pervert, eyes up!"

"No fair Psyche, it's been ages since I got me some boob; you've been away so long." Cupid pouted and

Psyche found it hard to stay mad. He was her husband, her extremely gorgeous and horny husband, but he had the attention span of a flea when it came to anything else other than love related subjects and as per his actions, he got bored easily. She had to force herself to concentrate as he continued his little rant.

"You left, and what did Pedro and I have to do besides sit and watch TV? Nothing." He pouted more. "I missed you, Wife."

He stepped forward, wrapped his arms around her waist and tugged her into his hot and hard body. Her own reacted as it always did, but she placed her hands on his chest and halted his assault. Distraction would not work on her this time.

"Cupid? Did you use the Essence?" she asked calmly, her eyes on his face. His blue eyes once had hypnotised her and lead her on a merry chase, but now she had the ability to resist.

"Cupid," she prompted, and was rewarded with a whispered answer.

"Yes?"

"Are you kidding me?" she shouted as she stepped away from his embrace, and he bent his head. "My love, you know what happens when you use that."

"It worked fine the last time, boo boo."

Psyche growled as he said the last nickname. He

had many for her, but this one always made her a tad irate

"For the last time, I am not a fucking bear, Cupid. You really need to stop watching those kids programs. And the reason it worked last time was because you had left it with only a few drops in. Marcella didn't wear the damn stuff."

Psyche paced the room, being careful to avoid knocking down any mortals as she did. She walked over to the bar and stood in front of the mortal that had been the recipient of Cupid's help.

She was stood on the bar and had a broom handle in her hand. Men surrounded her, all with adoration pasted across their faces as they tried to touch her. They had already from the looks of her torn skirt. Her facial expression was priceless; a warrior battling an army as she wielded her broom.

Psyche scrubbed a hand down her face and after looking at the mortal, she turned to face Cupid again, only to find his eyes glued to her arse.

"Focus!" she shouted, and watched as he jumped. "What happened when you used it before Marcella, Cupid?"

She watched again as he winced and started to look sheepish. His lack of willpower, as well as lack of control, was one of the reasons they had granted her immortality; as she seemed to be the only one able to control his "asshat" tendencies. That was until she had gone away.

"Cupid, the last time you let that spell loose it was with Cleopatra, and look how that ended." He winced again and nodded.

"I know."

"You know? And yet you let it loose on a modern mortal. Honey, they are even less prepared for it than the ancient mortals were. At least they believed in magic." She waved her hand about. "These don't, they believe in only what they can see."

Psyche walked over to Cupid and cupped his face in her palms, bringing his face up and his eyes to meet her own.

"My love," she said sweetly. "You fucked up big time." She sighed, kissed his lips and stepped away. "So, what are we going to do about it?"

†

Cupid smiled at his wife, even after all this time she could distract him with a single look; pull him to her with just a crook of her finger. But she was right, as usual, he thought. He had well and truly fucked up, as was evident by the horny males trying to climb the bar and get to his chosen mortal. Cupid's answer to Psyche about what to do was not going to gain him any man points. In fact, it may well just put him in the red completely.

"We can't stop it," he replied, and watched as her eyes widened with panic as she looked back to the mortal who was mid battle on the bar.

"What do you mean we can't stop it, Cupid? She's going to get ravished!"

"You like getting ravished," he answered back quickly, and was rewarded with a growl and a smack upside of his head.

"Owie baby, that hurt!"

"Get over it. And I only like getting ravished by you, dickhead. I don't think she wants to get ravished by multiple men, in a bar, in front of everyone, do you?"

"Err… no," he replied.

"So what the fuck do we do, brains? This is your doing, so bloody sort it," she shouted again. It took everything he had to stop staring at Psyche's breasts, they were perfection after all and *Pedro* had missed her so.

"Cupid!" she shouted again. Fuck, he thought, busted.

"Fine," he called and started to pace in front of

his wife, thinking hard about his little spell and how to fix his "fuck up", as his wife had called it.

"Aha!" he shouted and stood in the middle of the room, hands on his hips. "I have it."

"Go on," Psyche said as she walked over to an empty stool and perched on it.

"She has to admit who has her heart. One of the males around here owns it or the spell wouldn't be as potent. She just hasn't admitted it yet, as soon as she does… poof!" Cupid said poof at the same time he did a poof like gesture with his hands.

"Poof?" Psyche repeated.

"Yes, poof. All these males will forget their intense ardour for our mortal and she will be free of the spell and the bottle, well, that's if it is the Essence that has made shit go batshit crazy." Cupid frowned as he remembered the words spoken by a certain god not long ago. "That could be it," he finished, but didn't mention his meeting with Apollo straight away.

"So where is the mortal she loves, Cupid?"

"Err, that would be the question I can't answer my love. Can I get a kiss now?"

"No."

"No?" he repeated.

"NO, and you know why?"

Cupid shook his head and pouted. On most men

that would look ridiculous, but on him it just looked cute and slightly sexy.

"There is a major problem with your plan my love."

"What's that, love blossom?" he purred, totally unfazed by the total shit storm he had stirred up. Pysche's face, although serene, her eyes fired showing just how annoyed she really was. Cupid knew she was classed as his keeper and then one that had to clean his shit up when he made slight miscalculations.

"She won't be able to admit who has her heart. She won't even be able to say she loves him. Not yet anyway. These modern mortals are stubborn, my love. They have to get to know one another before they will even contemplate the notion of love. They have forgotten how to listen to their hearts and souls."

Cupid didn't like the frown that marred his wife's beautiful face. He much preferred her open mouthed after an orgasm. But thinking about that would just distract him again. He knew he had a short attention span, he couldn't help it. It was in his nature, but he hated knowing he had put Pysche in such a position.

"Cupid, we have to find another way. Try and find the mortal male before she," Psyche pointed at the female, "is ceased upon by every bloody male in this room, or else Pedro won't get to visit his favourite garden ever again." She paused, her own eyes filled with love for him but also annoyance. "Do I make myself clear?"

"Yes, sexy pants."

"And Cupid?"

"Yes stroodle?" he answered.

"Hurry up, because I have missed Pedro…a lot."

She smiled, blew him a kiss and vanished.

"See, told ya she missed us Pedro." Cupid patted his bulge before he turned and left the room, the mannequin challenge still in place. As he did, he pulled out his own phone and sent a text to his wife. Yes, he had only just seen her but has he had stated, she had his balls in a sack and, as such, he felt he couldn't tell her he had met Apollo in person. So instead, he sent a text and hoped she may just well take the hint.

Chapter Twenty-Three

Belinda's hands felt sore from wielding the broom but as soon as she had managed to knock a few out, she took the chance to jump through the gap in the pumps and into the service area. She could still hear the grunts from the fight and some of the men calling for her to go back, but she ignored them and found her way to the back door that led through the kitchen and then out into the rear beer garden.

The sooner she was out the sooner she could call Mike and tell him… What should she tell him? She couldn't exactly say the whole bar had gone mental over her, that would make her sound like a right stuck up cow.

Shit, shit, shit, that was all that was going through her mind, that and the fact some twatknuckle had ripped her skirt trying to get his meaty paws on her. Why had they gone all bloody handsy all of a sudden? Belinda thought, as she pushed open the back door with more force than she thought, and nearly got it back in the face when it hit the wall and swung back.

"What the hell?" she cried and dived out of the way, her boots slipping on the wet grass and sending her to the floor. The air shot from her lungs and pain shot up her knees as they connected with the earth. Yes, it was damp, but the floor was almost like concrete from the recent freezing weather.

What a disaster of an evening, and she had never even met up with Mike. That probably disappointed her the most. She had been so excited about the date, well, that along with the nerves. Yes, she had been early but even after the brawl had started she still hadn't seen him, and he had been late then.

"That's it, I've had enough of tonight. I'm going home."

She growled into the darkness and pushed to her feet, her jeans were damp, her knees hurt and her hands now sported some cracking scratches. But it was nothing a hot bath and her bed wouldn't solve.

"Ahh Belinda, here you are," the familiar voice called out from the dark, before a lone figure stepped out of the shadows from the side of the building. There was little light with the garden not being used, so all she could see was a shadow.

"Who's there?" she called out and wiped her hands down her jeans as she peered into the shadows.

After a moment of silence, she watched Clint step into the light. She couldn't forget his face or name, especially after the way he had spoken to her in the library earlier that day. A shiver creeped up her spine as he approached, a strange smile on his face. He looked familiar but also looked strange. Belinda didn't know if it was her imagination, but his eyes seemed to glow.

"Why are you out here all alone Belinda?" The way he said her name gave her the creeps and she couldn't help the involuntary step back. "I thought you would be enjoying the attention in the bar, all those men flocking to you."

His eyes weren't the only thing that seemed creepy, his voice seemed to vibrate and echo with a secondary tone, it was if there were two voices in one. "Isn't that what you wanted? Isn't that why you have the Essence?"

Belinda frowned, no one knew about the Essence. So how did Clint?

"Excuse me?" she replied. She was going to act dumb. She didn't know what he wanted with the Essence but she had a feeling it wasn't good, so keeping shtum about it would be the best course of action. This time, though, she stood her ground when he stepped closer, but she felt a trickle of fear seep into her thin courage.

"The Essence, Belinda dear, you no longer need it. I don't think whoring yourself out will be hard, especially with an arse like yours."

Belinda was stunned at the blatant rudeness of a man she had only met the once. Letting instinct take over, her hand shot out and connected with his cheek as hard as she could. Her hand instantly started to sting but she didn't care. She was no whore and for him to state it was rude and disrespectful.

"I don't know who the fuck you think you are, but I am no whore. I'm leaving." Belinda turned to walk past and only got a foot if that before Clint's hand shot out and caught her across the cheek.

Before she was able to react, his hand once again shot out and grabbed her by the throat. She clawed at the flesh in an attempt for him to release her but instead, he turned them both and walked her back to the rear wall of the building, slamming her back into the brick.

Belinda was no delicate flower and knew her weight wasn't slight, so when her feet left the ground she knew she was in trouble. His fingers dug into the skin of her neck and would leave clear, bright marks if he ever released her. Instead, he leaned forward and growled in a voice that was no longer Clint's but something else entirely.

"Stupid mortal, you dare mess with a god. Your death will not be quick and you will tell me where the Essence is. I know you have it, your aura reeks of Cupid's handy work."

Clint smiled and then sniffed, "Yes, Cupid and another male have got their grips on you Belinda."

Belinda started to struggle, although the ability to breathe was becoming harder and harder each second. Clint squeezed harder as he slammed her head back into the bricks and caused stars to erupt behind her eyes. As darkness started to impede on her vision, she heard his words.

"Know this, mortal; you will fear me, then you will die."

Chapter Twenty-Four

Aphrodite lounged in her temple and flicked through her shiny new phone that she had finally been taught how to use. She was still slow, but she was sure it wouldn't take her long, especially if everyone left her alone to play.

It seemed to be the day where every being on Olympus wanted her and she was supposed to be on holiday with the girls. The only reason she was back was because poor Psyche had looked especially stressed when she had left to check on her unruly husband and according to some, her apparent son. That was if you believed all that the mortal history books said, when in fact, it was about as incorrect as you could get.

She shuddered at the thought of being the one to produce Cupid. Besides the fact he was created fully grown, she was careful when it came to the whole subject of children.

Cupid's existence had been purely by accident and

was a product of a time when she was, you could say, stressed to the eyeballs. In the early days of being a Goddess, when Zeus had first taken charge, she had become overwhelmed with the world's needs and prayers for love and had nearly drowned under the weight.

Still new to her extended powers, she had tried to create something that would help her with the demand and as such, created Cupid. The problem was, as he learned and was unleashed on the world his helpfulness had reduced and he had become more and more like the Norse god, Loki. He was more intent on being personally involved in the mortal's lives and had caused a great many disasters. The Helen of Troy situation and the Cleopatra one were classic examples. The situations would put them, as Hermes would say, "Up shit creak without a paddle".

So they had tried to stop him and that had not worked out well, he fought every attempt to bind his powers and it had taken the help of a mortal girl to stop him. As a thank you, and for the future control of Cupid, Psyche had been made immortal. She was Cupid's match in every way and was now the only one capable of controlling him.

How he had found her, Aphrodite didn't know. But one minute he was placing love spells on horses and the next he was throwing gifts galore at a mortal woman. That right there had shown Aphrodite even the gods needed and craved true love. They felt just as much and as hard as mortals did, and it was now her job to make sure they got the chance. The rest was up to them.

The phone vibrated in her hand and caused her to scream and drop it onto the cushions.

"My lady, are you well?" A small nymph rushed into the room.

"Yes, yes I am fine, these mortal toys are taking some getting used to."

The nymph nodded and bowed, ready to leave the room.

"Don't leave just yet, I may have need of you. Just let me figure out how to open this."

Aphrodite bit her lip in concentration as she managed to open the phone screen and read the text that had come through.

Aphrodite

Cupid has fucked up...big style. I think I'm going to need some help with this one.

He didn't have the balls to tell me, but he's spoken to Apollo.

Isn't he in the underworld????
Shit is going down in London, hon, hurry.
Pxx

The goddess of love stood up in a rush and nearly fell back down as the blood rushed south and caused her to go dizzy.

"My lady?" the nymph once again questioned.

"I'm good, please hurry to Elyssia and inform Hades his presence is required."

"He isn't there my lady."

"What? What do you mean he isn't there?"

"He left a note after you had left with the other goddess'" the nymph answered and handed over the hand written note.

Goddess, I have taken your advice and I have decided to visit the mortal realm and try to woo my intended. Worry not for I will succeed.
Hades.

"Ahh crap," Aphrodite mumbled, her mind raced to form a plan of action.

"Ok, please fetch Hermes and inform him he is to fetch Hades from his date and bring him to…" Aphrodite looked at her phone, "London, bring him to London and if he argues, inform him his charge seems to have found a way to get out."

Aphrodite watched as the nymph hurried away with her message. If Psyche was right, along with Cupid, then things would have to change soon. That god had been left unpunished for too long and something would need to be done before it was too late.

Chapter
Twenty-Five

Mike was late, really late, but it was something he was unable to avoid. His friend, Gary, had decided to rock up and wouldn't leave and then wouldn't shut up. Mike then had to admit that he had a date, but that opened up more questions and by that point, Mike was ready to gag his mate and leave him tied up in his kitchen. In the end, he had left him with the TV remote and told him to use the spare room. Mike would, if he was lucky, be going back to Belinda's to finish what they started or to just carry on doing what they had done, but with more contact and less clothing.

He smiled as he remembered every detail of the afternoon, she was so damn beautiful and it would be nice to sit and have a proper conversation with her as well. To him, she was the complete package and he couldn't wait to start showing her that there was more to him than a mechanic and a tank build.

As he walked into *The Vicar's Pulpit*, he didn't

expect to see it in a full out brawl; tables were broken and upended and chairs had been thrown against the wall. Bodies lay scattered, battered but alive, but there was no sign of Belinda. His heart shot into his mouth at the thought of her being hurt. Mike started to battle his way through the pub.

"Belinda," he called out as he stepped over men he had drunk with multiple times, until he found the barman curled in a corner, arms over his head.

"Barry, you ok man?"

"No mate, this place is mental."

"What happened?" Mike asked as he helped the man up off the floor.

"Not sure, but everything kicked off after a woman came up to the bar. One minute she had ordered a drink the next… every guy in the place was trying to pay for it and then boom! It all went mental."

"Woman? Where did she go Barry, what happened to her?"

"I think she went out back dude, she was on the bar with the broom at one point."

Mike didn't wait to hear anything else and bolted for the back door, concern for Belinda growing with every second. Quietly he pushed open the door and stepped out into the dark, his eyes quickly adjusting to the dim light. He was only just able to see the outline of two figures by the wall. On the first glance, it looked as though a couple were getting up close and personal, until Mike heard a muffled cry.

As he got closer he saw Belinda against the wall, almost unconscious at the hands of Clint. Mike growled and dived, taking hold of Clint at the waist and lifting him off the ground. He pushed him forward then tipped him over and slammed him into the floor.

On the rugby pitch that move would have got him the red card but right now, it helped deliver some damage and helped direct his rage. He left Clint winded upon the floor and turned back to help Belinda. As he approached, she dived back against the wall, fear etched across her face.

"Shhh baby, it's me, it's ok." Her eyes changed from blind panic to recognition and she slowly got to her feet. Mike clenched his fists as he saw the deep purple bruises that marred the skin of her neck and she was wheezing for breath. He reached out and traced the skin gently before pulling her into his arms.

"Oh Mike!" she cried out. "I was so scared, I couldn't breathe and he just kept squeezing." She sobbed into his shirt, her body shaking and he rubbed his hands gently up and down her back.

"Aww, well ain't this cute?" Clint's voice called from behind.

"Fuck off, Clint, before I dump you on your arse again," Mike responded. Releasing Belinda from the cage of his arms, he turned but kept her behind him and faced Clint.

"You can try," Clint said and just smiled as he levelled a small revolver on Mike's chest. "Belinda! Oh Belinda, come out, come out," he called in a sing-song voice that held a hint of crazy about it.

"Leave her out of this." Mike held up his hands and took a step closer.

"No can do, she knows what I want and unless she hands it over, I will empty this gun into your chest," Clint said with a smirk, as his other hand pulled out a serrated blade and waved it at them.

"No, don't, "Belinda called as she stepped out from behind Mike's huge frame. "I will give you what you want," she said, but was stopped from moving forward by Mike's trunk like arm.

"Stay back baby, I don't trust him," Mike growled out. "Don't give him anything, he's obviously lost it."

"It's ok, I don't want you hurt Mike," she said and smiled up at him as she squeezed his arm. At any other time he would be overjoyed at the fact she wanted to protect him but right now, it was his job to protect her. Belinda stepped past him once more. Mike watched and followed close behind. He would wait for a chance to deal with Clint but only if Belinda wasn't in the firing line.

Her shaky hand reached into her handbag and pulled out a small wooden box. Mike had no clue what was in it or why it was so damn important that a guy would lose his marbles over it, but at the same time he was so proud of Belinda as she stood tall and faced Clint, holding out the box for him to take. He could tell she was shaking, a full body shiver seem to take over her so he closed the distance, just so he could touch her and reassure her that he was there.

Clint's eyes were wild and unfocused as he grabbed the box with the same hand that gripped the knife and lowered the one that held the gun. Mike saw his chance.

He pushed Belinda out of the way and stormed forward, knocking the gun from his hand and punching Clint in the jaw. The gunshot that went off luckily missed him and Belinda, but echoed in the night making Belinda scream in terror.

Mike felt like he had punched concrete as Clint fired back with his own not so meaty fist. The box and knife forgotten, Mike went full tilt into the fight, taking punches that, if they kept up, would knock him out sooner rather than later. As they fell to the ground, Mike pinned Clint but kept punching him continuously in his face. The sound of flesh and bone crunching was all that could be heard.

"Mike stop, please stop, he's had enough," Belinda pleaded and tried to pull Mike from a prone Clint. He stopped his punching and looked up into the tear streak faced of his girl. Yes, she was his; she always had been.

"He hurt you baby, I can't have that." He was honest with his answer, now that she had a glimpse of the anger he usually kept a tight rein on.

"He's finished," she whispered. "You saved me, ok?" She smiled and he felt himself fall. Yes, he had a soft and tender side and she tapped into it every fucking time. He would do anything for her. That, he thought, he had just proven.

"Baby, let's…"

"Mike!!" He heard Belinda call his name, felt pain shoot through his stomach. He looked down to see the hilt of a knife, the blade buried into his gut as Clint started to laugh through battered lips.

"You lose, mortal," Clint said, and Mike swore he saw his eyes turn gold as he was pushed to the side.

Belinda's cry echoed in his ears as he hit the cold, wet floor.

✝

Belinda watched Clint stab Mike as if in slow motion. She'd watched him grab the knife from where it had landed on the grass. He had grinned as he had pushed slowly through the flesh of Mike's stomach, as if it gave him pure pleasure to inflict pain. Belinda hadn't been able to stop the scream that had erupted like an air siren from her throat. Her heart had dropped at the same time that Mike had fallen to the side, his hand gripping the hilt of the knife.

She had frozen in shock as Clint climbed to hit feet. He delivered a hard kick to Mike's back, in turn, causing a loud moan of pain.

She was petrified; she never in her entire life had expected something like this to happen to her and in this town. This was something you only ever saw on the news and never thought it would be real. It wasn't just that Clint had gone crazy, it was the fact he had enjoyed what he was doing to Mike. He seemed to enjoy inflicting pain on others.

Even when he had her by her throat he had

smiled, almost laughed even. She couldn't fathom how any creature could enjoy hurting another.

As she watched his continuous taunts and punishment to Mike's already felled form, she felt a bubble of anger start in the pit of her stomach. It slowly festered until it became a raging boil. This man had ruined her chance at happiness with Mike. Her heart was in pieces now. Even though they hadn't spent as much time together as she had wanted, she could honestly say she felt intense emotion towards him and that was enough, as she had never ever felt that towards anyone else.

Belinda's eyes scanned the grass and quickly spotted the wooden box that housed the Essence, but next to it was the gun that had been dropped when Mike had attacked. Silly man, he shouldn't have done that. But to know he had done that just to protect her, made her want to cry.

Slowly she bent and reached out for the gun, palming the cool metal in her hand. She kept her eyes on Clint and had to stop herself from wincing with each kick he delivered to Mike's back, no doubt worsening the wound he had. She had no idea how to use a gun, this was the first ever time she had picked one up and it felt wrong in her hand. Going on instinct and what she had seen on the TV, she pulled back the cock on the revolver and held it up, pointed straight at Clint.

"Stop it!" she screeched out. Panic had started as Mike was no longer moving. "Stop it right now or I will blow your goddamn head off." She was bluffing, she didn't even know if she would hit Clint, but she hoped the threat would work.

Instead, Clint kicked Mike one last time then walked around him. His battered face was almost unrecognisable, but his eyes now glowed bright with a gold hue.

"What are you?" Belinda whispered.

Clint walked around Mike's body and towards the wooden box. He bent and collected it and then stood confidently in front of Belinda, as if unafraid of the gun she held.

"What am I? Now that is a good question. You mortals are so close-minded and you never think outside of the box." Clint sighed. "Clint here was easy to control, his thoughts were already corrupt; wanting things he shouldn't." Clint laughed, "Oh I am sorry, my dear." He smiled again then bowed.

"My name is Apollo, lord and god of the sun."

Belinda's mouth opened… a god. But then, she shouldn't really be surprised, after all, she did have a bottle named Cupid's Essence in her handbag.

"I see you are struck dumb by my mere presence. Please forgive my appearance. Clint is not as handsome as my true form." He started to babble, seemingly to enjoy the sound of his own voice, as he passed the wooden box from one hand to the other. "I had great power but it was taken from me, and this…" He held up the box, "will help restore what is rightfully mine and help me seek my vengeance." With that said, Apollo/Clint opened the wooden box. His face instantly changed, his smile gone and instead replaced by a sneer. Hate filled his golden eyes.

"Where is it?" he shouted, and threw the empty wooden box to the floor.

Belinda stood her ground, both hands gripped the gun and it still shook. Clint/Apollo's faced morphed with rage, scaring her more than anything she had seen before. He stepped close; his large hand reached out and once again gripped her throat.

"I WANT THE ESSENCE!"

BOOM!!

The sound of the gunshot echoed once again through the empty garden and Belinda opened her eyes, not even realising that she had closed them when she had pressed her finger to the trigger and pulled.

Clint's/Apollo's eyes dimmed from gold, back to

the dull grey and his shocked face turned slack as he slid to the floor at Belinda's feet. She could hear the sound of his chest as it wheezed in and out in an attempt to get air into his lungs.

With him forgotten, Belinda rushed to Mike's side. Falling to her knees, she dropped the gun and she pulled his head onto her lap.

"Mike, honey, please open your eyes, look at me." No answer, his eyes fluttered and his breathing was shallow, but he didn't wake. She couldn't stop the sobbing once it had started. She pulled at her jacket and pressed it into the wound which was now free from the knife. The multiple kicks had knocked it free and Mike was now losing a lot of blood.

"You can't leave me Mike, not when we've just found each other," she sobbed. "Don't go, Mike!"

Belinda looked around her, before screaming for help. She had dropped her handbag after Clint had attacked her, so she couldn't get to her mobile.

"PLEASE! ANYONE? HELP ME!" She called into the night, her heart already knowing Mike didn't have much chance.

Chapter
Twenty-Six

Cupid watched, stunned at the scene that had just unfolded. It was hard to believe that in the space of only half an hour, his mortal had gone from being on her first proper date to now firing a gun in self-defence. It all seemed to happen in slow motion; the fight, the screams and then the gunshot. Cupid had always prided himself on being a selfish bastard, but seeing the mortal female scream in terror and react like a fecking soldier both scared him and made him a tad proud.

Hades still had hold of both of his arms, stopping him from entering the fray. The minute shit had gone down, Cupid had wanted to step in and save Belinda. He frowned, when had he learned her name? That was unusual in itself, but the fear that was all over her face now as she ignored the fallen Clint and rushed to be by Mike's side, pulled at the heart strings he never knew he had, until Psyche.

Cupid looked to his wife, seeing her hugging

Aphrodite. Both had streams of tears that ran down their beautiful faces as they too watched the battle that had occurred.

He looked again back towards where the mortals were lay sprawled upon the grass out the back of the pub. There were benches dotted around and a small climbing frame. The area would be lovely in the summer but now, in the dark, in the cold, it was creepy.

Belinda's weeping filled the silence and Cupid focused his senses on the two fallen males. He didn't think Clint had suffered a mortal wound but it had done its job in stopping him, that and the damage it had done had also expelled Apollo's presence from the unknowing male and sent him back to his prison in the underworld.

That god, if he had his way, would be punished severely for what he had done here, that and his actions to others. Cupid shook his head and pulled his arms free of Hades.

"Get the fuck off," he growled out and walked towards his wife, taking her in his arms and pressing a kiss to her forehead. "I'm sorry," he whispered, well aware that some of the blame was his. This always happened when he got involved. Cupid just didn't seem to learn the lesson; this time he would.

He didn't wait for a reply from Psyche; instead, he walked towards where Belinda sat in the wet grass cradling Mike's head in her lap as she pressed her jacket into his wound.

Clint had pulled a serrated kitchen knife from somewhere when Mike had appeared and knocked the gun from his hand. He could see Belinda was doing little to stop the blood flow that pulsed from his body. Her hands were too small and the jacket being made of faux leather wasn't exactly amazing at staunching the blood flow.

But what broke his heart now, was hearing a battered and bruised Belinda sob as she held Mike's head in her lap. Her cries hurt him, actually made his heart feel like it was about to break and for all of her efforts, he knew there was little she could do to stop the inevitable.

"Help them for fucks sake," he growled out, he couldn't- no, he wouldn't watch this happen. "Surely we owe the two mortals this much." He turned towards his fellow gods, his voice on the verge of begging.

"Cupid, you know the rules," Hades deep voice called out from the shadows. Even dressed in mortal clothing he could vanish into the dark.

"Oh fuck off with your rules, Hades. We both

know they mean jack shit these days." Cupid had had it with rules and what you can and can't do. So he turned to the one person who may actually be on his side in all of this. He looked at Aphrodite and clasped his hands together. This time he did beg.

"Please help them. You know I don't have that power."

"Goddess," Hades called out, his tone set as a warning. But he was stopped from speaking by the upraised, perfectly manicured hand of Aphrodite. Cupid grinned, seeing her act all rebellious gave him a hint to where some of his traits came from and not just because he was an arsehole.

"Hades, shut up, I swear you have a skull made from granite. Have you seriously not listened to anything I have said recently?"

She shook her head and waved both hands in front of her as she mumbled about mens inability to listen, he owes her shit etc., the list went on. In the end, Cupid had to turn away, her mumbles were distracting and they had a job to do.

That and the God of the underworld had a lot to deal with back in his plain. Somehow, Apollo had gained the ability to effect the mortals from his prison. Cupid would happily volunteer to help beat some sense into that prick, but that would have to wait until later.

Just as it had happened in the pub, when Psyche had busted him and the Essence had gone a little bit mental, time stopped. Belinda's cries of sorrow and anguish went silent and all movement, but for that of the gods, stopped. The silence was deafening and Cupid didn't like it, which was one of the reasons he preferred living on the mortal plain; Olympus was too quiet.

He watched as the Goddess of Love and his creator stepped forward, her power pulsed as she whispered her sacred words. Not many got to witness the true power of love and it was a sight to behold.

Where Cupid's power was a pale pink, Aphrodite's was deep red with hints of purples and pinks. In his creator's presence, he felt his own power pick up as if trying to merge and return.

"Cupid, lock your power away, I would hate to drain you of it," she called out, just as she bent her head. Her words were strong and echoed in the silence. "I will not heal him completely, the mortals would never understand. But I will stop the bleeding enough so the ambulance can arrive in time and he can be healed their way."

Cupid nodded and looked at his mortal; tears

stained her face, along with a brutal bruise across her cheek where Apollo had struck her. That's when he had gone a little bit batshit mental himself. That had been when Hades had had to restrain him. If there was one thing that got him riled up, it was violence on women

"My love," Psyche whispered as her hands rested on his shoulders, squeezing reassuringly. "I have called for an ambulance. All will be well my love, but we need to leave, now."

She rested her head on his shoulder as they watched Aphrodite finish with her spell and step back towards Hades.

"Go," he said sternly and turned to kiss Psyche on the lips. "I will return when I know my interference hasn't caused permanent damage." He smiled, only a slight tilt of the lips that told her it would be ok, but this was something he had to do on his own. The voices of the gods became almost forgotten as he walked back towards the frozen couple.

"Come Hades, let us have a chat," Aphrodite called out to Hades in an almost teacher/student kind of way.

"What about, Aphrodite? I am doing everything you said." Hades said sulkily.

"You, my lord, don't listen."

A bright flash of light signalled the departure of the gods, neither one asking for thanks, and neither one would get it. The mortals deserved their help, it was the least they could have done. Cupid was left in the dark alone and ready, for once, to take responsibility for his actions as time returned to normal. The god of love changed to that of an old gentleman bending to help Belinda as the ambulance arrived, just as promised by Psyche. All would be well; he would make sure of it.

Chapter
Twenty-Seven

Belinda smiled at the old man as he wrapped a blanket around her shoulders and handed her, her handbag. He had been the only one to respond to her cry for help, but his swift action may have just saved Mike's life. The paramedics had stabilised him on the grass and were now transferring him to the ambulance. They had been quick to put her at ease when she was convinced that he had gone. Whatever she had done with her jacket, it had stopped the bleeding long enough that, when they had arrived, they could patch him up until they could get Mike into surgery.

"Miss? Can I get you anything else?" the old gentleman asked.

Belinda shook her head and watched the paramedics wheel Mike into the back of the ambulance. She was unable to accompany them in the ambulance and the police wanted to question her about what had happened.

"No thank you, but thank you so much for your help."

"Not a bother Miss, you need me just call, ok?" He smiled and waddled off into the pub.

She couldn't seem to turn her mind off from what had happened and was unsure exactly what to tell the police, other than Clint going crazy and attacking her. She couldn't very well say that he had been possessed by an ancient Greek god who harboured plans of vengeance. Even that seemed farfetched and if she hadn't of just been through it, she would have never believed it.

Picking up her handbag, Belinda went through it to find her phone along with the bottle that had been the cause of the havoc that had occurred, only to find it missing. Frowning, she got to her feet and paced around the grass where it had been and where the box had been thrown, only to find them both missing. Strange, she thought. But did she really need them now?

"Miss Adams?" an officer called as they sent Clint off in another ambulance. When she had shot him she had, of course, closed her eyes and the shot had gone into his shoulder and not his chest. Still, she had done enough to stop him and now he was handcuffed and would be dealt with by the police.

"Yes officer?" Belinda said and tried not to wince as her voice croaked. Her throat hurt, as was expected.

"Would you like to accompany me to the hospital where we can get you looked at, and also, we will need to take a statement."

"Yes, of course." Belinda nodded and followed the officer to the car park, she would be happy when she could go home. Go home and try to forget this whole ordeal.

This night couldn't end quickly enough.

†

Mike opened his eyes and then closed them again instantly. The bright lights gave him an instant headache. Every muscle in his body ached and his stomach felt like he had been ripped apart.

"Shit, that hurts," Mike cried out as he tried to move, only to set off a round of beeping. When he opened his eyes, he found himself on a hospital bed hooked up to a multitude of machines. With each movement more and more alarms reacted until a nurse finally entered the room to turn them off.

"Sir, please don't tug at the lines."

"Where the hell am I?" he grumbled out as he was

pushed back onto his back. She ignored his question as she checked his vitals and then worked on switching off the monitors.

"Lady, what the hell happened?" Mike had a total mind blank and whenever he tried to think about the last thing he could remember, his headache got worse.

"Just a second sir, now you are awake I will fetch your girlfriend; she hasn't left your side since you came in."

Girlfriend? Since when did he have a girlfriend? He would surely remember that. Instead of questioning it, he kept quiet and waited for the nurse to leave the room.

Mike closed his eyes and rested his head back against the pillows and tried to think, but everything just seemed a blur.

"Mike?" a soft voice called and he opened his eyes once more. There stood a beautiful woman with long, dark hair and hypnotic eyes, but… why couldn't he remember her name or who she was?

"Hi," he croaked out, his voice just as husky as hers. It was then, as she approached, he noticed the large black/green bruise that covered her left cheek and the deep purple marks that covered her neck.

"What the hell happened to you?" he blurted out.

She blushed as she sat on the edge of his bed and

took his hand, stroking the skin. She seemed so focused on his hand that she didn't answer. Until a quiet voice, followed by tear filled eyes, pulled his attention.

"I was convinced I had lost you Mike. When he stabbed you I thought that was it."

Mike didn't reply, but that snippet of information answered the question as to why he felt like his insides had been put in a blender.

As he looked at her beautiful face, a string of images flashed through his mind and made the headache ten times worse.

"Ahhh shit," he called out as he threw his hands to his head, cupping it in an effort to fight the pain. Every image of him and the lady together played out in his head. Every feeling he felt, everything he said slowly filtered back in, leading up until the attack and the stabbing.

"Belinda," he whispered as he fought the pain.

"Mike, are you ok?" she asked and he felt her soft hands on his own.

"Belinda…Oh god, Belinda!" Mike pulled her arms and pulled her up and over his lap, regardless of the wires and the pain his stomach was in.

"Fuck, baby. How did you get away, what happened?" He stroked the bruise on her face and then the ones on her neck, feeling himself get angry all over again.

"I shot him, Mike."

"You what?" He was stunned, feelings of pride and affection coursed through him, this woman was simply amazing. She continued on with her story, showing just how much of a warrior his girl truly was.

"I shot him. He kept kicking you after he had stabbed you and I got so angry I just… pulled the trigger." She had started to sob as she relived what had happened. He pulled her closer and laid small kisses upon her temple.

"I was so scared Mike, scared for you," she sobbed out and then looked up into his eyes. God, she was stunning even after she had been crying. Cupping her face, he smiled back.

"Baby, I don't think anything could keep us apart now, do you?" He grinned as she shook her head and reached up to grab his face, her hands fluttering across his cheeks.

"No Mike, I've decided to keep you."

"Oh I like the sound of that, baby," he chuckled and leaned his head back against the pillows and pulled her tight against him. A feeling of exhaustion had started to set in but he was determined not let her go; not now, not ever. It had taken long enough to get her in his arms. He wanted to know what had gone on after he had lost consciousness so without stalling, he asked. "What happened to Clint baby, tell me?"

He felt her snuggle into him and he relaxed as he listened.

"He was arrested for attempted murder on you and attacking me. He was also investigated for stalking."

"Stalking?" Mike asked. "Really?"

"Yeah," Belinda admitted as she pressed her face into his chest. "Mike, Clint had been following me for months. The police checked out his home and found that he had pictures of me and had been buying items, like the gun and other stuff." He felt her shiver against him.

"They said he had been under the care of a psychologist but had gone AWOL from his care centre."

"It's ok now baby, he won't hurt you anymore." Mike used his fingers to tilt Belinda's face towards his and changed the subject once again, this time to more positive news.

"So, you are my girlfriend now, eh?" he asked with a grin.

Belinda countered but she was also smiling. "Well, they wouldn't let me in otherwise."

"I like the sound of that, it means you are mine," Mike admitted.

"I like being yours, Mike," she answered with a blush. "But Mike?"

"Yeah baby," Mike mumbled as his lips skipped across her jaw line.

"What happened to your stutter?" she questioned.

"Baby, you wouldn't believe me if I told you," Mike responded, then fired one back. "Baby, what did Clint mean by the Essence?"

Belinda grinned and moved so her face was closer to his. "You wouldn't believe me if I told you," she repeated, then placed her lips on his. Mike wrapped his arms around his girl and ignored the alarms that kept going off at his side.

Finally, he thought, she was his. Finally.

✝

Cupid smiled as his two mortals kissed and got reacquainted. It had been a hard journey for both of them and if Cupid was honest, he *had* kinda messed things up. But that was what he did well.

Love wasn't meant to be easy, maybe that was why

he had been created; to remind people that love was hard and you had to work at it. Cupid moved away from the window of the hospital room and moved down the corridor. Although things had been looking dicey, everything had worked out just like he wanted. And the Essence? Well, that was back where it belonged. Hidden away and not to be used ever again. He had been worried that Belinda had really given it to Apollo but he had, as he had always done, underestimated the mortals.

But it had done its job.

The mortals had in fact gained their hearts desire.

Cupid grinned as he walked towards the exit of the hospital ward. He had one last thing to do before he went home, and this couldn't wait.

It was time for Cupid to be- well, Cupid.

Epilogue

Bob and Martha Daniels stood and smiled at each other as Bob reached over and pressed the large, lit button that would signal for the lift. They had spent the entire day shopping, not something Bob usually enjoyed but for his wife's birthday he would have endured anything. After their late meal out they were both now eager to return to their small third floor apartment to relax and have a warm cup of tea.

Martha squeezed Bob's hand gently as the doors to the lift slid open and they stepped inside. The interior was well lit, with a large mirror across the back wall. The signature *"ding"* was followed by the posh English accent of a woman who confirmed the lift's current location.

"*Ding-* Parking Level."

Bob pressed the button on the panel that was lit with a large number three and stepped to the side, pulling his wife with him. He wrapped his free arm around her small shoulders and kissed her head whilst he re-adjusted the grip he had on the multiple carrier bags from the shopping trip.

The door quietly slid shut and the lift gave a small lurch to signal its ascent. After 25 years of marriage, Bob was still madly in love with Martha and by the way she was smiling at him, it was plain as day she still felt the same.

Their lives had been filled with love and laughter, as well as the usual trials and tribulations that most couples go through throughout life, but to Bob they had the perfect marriage.

The lift came to a halt and once again the voice chimed above.

"*Ding-* Foyer."

A few seconds later the doors slid open to reveal the next person to enter the lift. Both Bob and Martha could do little but stare open-mouthed.

†

Cupid had pressed the button for the lift about ten or so times before it had finally opened and allowed him entrance. He swore it did it on purpose, you know; take its sweet damn time. Did it not realise who he was and what he had to do today? No of course not, it was a lift and, well, they didn't get out much, Cupid thought as he marched into the lift.

If he didn't get up to his home soon he would have no control over his actions. Yes, he had seen Psyche the other day but she hadn't exactly been "approachable" and she had even threatened *Pedro*.

Who the fuck does that, threatens a man's penis, his best friend and toy? It just wasn't right. But he was drawn to her like the proverbial moth to a flame or, in his terms, sausage to a roll. He snorted at his own joke; he was a funny bastard when he wanted to be. Maybe that would be his new venture- if Psyche would let him have his man card. A comedian, oh yes, but he would have to butter her up first.

Cupid had that niggling feeling, though, the buttering wouldn't be as easy as he hoped. Actually, he would bet Zeus's balls that she wouldn't be putting out for a while or returning his man card and balls either.

He had made a teeny, tiny mess… Cupid winced, ok it wasn't tiny, more like a monumental fuckup of epic proportions…but he had sorted it right. He nodded to himself.

"Yes, I fucking did."

"Excuse me?" the elderly male responded and

brought Cupid back from his inner conversation with himself. He had forgotten about the mortals.

"Sorry," he said, and then snapped his fingers as he realised the lift hadn't moved yet and the doors were still open.

"Ooops," he said with a grin and reached past both the mortals to press the button for the top floor. The female blushed bright red, as was usual when he was in the presence of a female. So he turned on the charm, winked and grinned more when she blushed even redder, but then turned her head into the shoulder of the male that had his arm protectively around her.

Cupid sighed, no matter the age they all wanted a piece of him. Not that he could blame them. Damn, even he got a little turned on when he looked at his reflection.

Cupid snorted and received another open-mouthed stare. Maybe he shouldn't have put Psyche's gift on before he got to the apartment, oh well.

Cupid leaned back on the wall at the back of the lift and folded his arms over his massive chest as he felt the lift move. Finally, he thought and let his mind continue his self-conversation. He found he could always make some sort of sense when he spoke to himself, and his jokes just cracked him up.

So the mess he had made, he had managed to clean up, with the encouragement of his wife and possibly the smallest bit of assistance from his…well, what do you call the woman that technically gave up a part of her power to create you but didn't actually give birth? Cupid tilted his head- auntie, let's call her his auntie, he thought and grinned. She would fucking hate that. He laughed and ignored the mortals as the lift stopped and they practically exited at speed. Shit, he wasn't scary was he? That wasn't the impression he was going for with the outfit.

Dammit, he wanted Psyche to flock to his side and beg to be bent over and…well, yeah, he thought. He knew where that little internal porn show was going. *Pedro* twitched in response to the fantasy.

"Soon my friend, soon." He patted his bulge and turned to face the mirror, his previous thoughts completely forgotten, as usual, and he looked over his current appearance.

He was pleased, no, scrap that, he was sodding ecstatic and it had taken him ages to find an outfit that fit. Most of the ones he had tried on had been for men not as well endowed as him, and there was no way on this earth he would subject *Pedro* to that sort of confinement. He didn't want anything to hinder his performance, and having the man berries strangled would most certainly mess with it. Although, he could play the sympathy vote with that one. Maybe next time.

As was the norm with Cupid, he was bare-chested and had even brushed his chest hair, making sure it was silky smooth and appealing. Along with the sparkly tinted moisturiser he had used, he believed it gave a brilliant effect. Instead of his grey joggers, Cupid now sported what most people would call an adult nappy, but was more loin cloth in design. That topped with some small wings on his back, a tiny quiver and a bow with an arrow topped with a love heart, it would take the dumbest asshat to not understand what he wanted to achieve with his outfit.

Cupid was dressed as Cupid. What woman would be able to resist?

"*Ding-* Top floor."

Cupid fluffed his hair and ran his hands seductively down his chest before he cupped his bulge and adjusted.

"Alright you sexy bastard, let's go."

He turned from the mirror and walked out into the hallway and toward the non-descript grey door of his and Psyche's home. Without knocking, he flung the door wide open.

"Snuggle bug, I'm home! I hope your clunge is moist as my sausage wants in its roll."

A high pitched female voice called out in response as the door slowly slid shut.

"What the fucking hell are you wearing Cupid? And did you really just say clu…"

Cupid and his wife were together once again and all was right in the world of the gods…or was it.

The End

Cupids Story

Pysche looked at the small white stick in her hand and back up to her reflection. She looked unusually pale for a goddess, but that's what you get when you team a nice bout of sickness with finding out you are pregnant. That and the fact the father is one of the most absent-minded gods to ever exist along with being a grade A fruitloop.

That didn't mean she didn't love him. Hell, she adored the idiot. But the whole idea of having a baby with him, of having a mini Cupid, actually sent shivers up her spine. She could honestly say she struggled with Cupid, but add a child into the mix would no doubt send her batshit crazy.

She again looked down at the white plastic pregnancy test in her hand and glared at the two red lines that bisected the small window. Amazing how two simple red lines could fuck up your day. Well, that and Cupid's "Super sperm".

Pysche turned away from the large gilded mirror

and sat on the toilet seat. She ignored the splendour that was the bathroom, she ignored the running water from the tap, she even ignored the light tapping that had started at the bathroom door from a certain god who she would blame for the whole thing.

Pysche may be a goddess but she was no way equipped to deal with being pregnant. That thought alone sent her memories spiralling backwards, recalling those days as a mortal and her first meeting with Cupid. She had been pregnant then, but that had ended in a completely different manner. She closed her eyes and leaned her head back on the cool tile and became lost in the memories.

Memories of being pursued by a god. Memories of Cupid's Beginning.

A Note From Jenn

So Cupid is finished and what can I say? Considering this book started off as a one line idea I am so happy with the outcome. Cupid has been both a pain in the arse and an absolute joy to write. He is a complete idiot but I love him.

So to answer the question that I am sure is flying around your head right now-YES, Cupid will have his very own book.

Well, as long as he behaves himself.

Thank you once again for the love and support, it means the world to me. Every review, every like on my page makes me smile.

Thank you
Love
Jenn

Xx

More From J Thompson

SoulKiss(Book 1 Soulmate Series)

SoulFate(Book 2 Soulmate Series)

SoulDeath (Book 3 Soulmate Series-March 2017)

Exercise in Love (Stand alone)

www.ingramcontent.com/pod-product-compliance
Lightning Source LLC
Chambersburg PA
CBHW070436120726
47910CB00003B/808